MAKENZI

UNEXPECTED

Truth

Published by
VYSS Publishing

ISBN-13: 978-0-9898910-0-4

Library of Congress Control Number: 2013915688

Printed in the United States of America

10 9 8 7 6 5 4 3 2 1

OTHER TITLES BY MAKENZI

Dangerously

That's How I Like It

Blood Brothers

Tanya,
① truly appreciate
the support, it
means alot

Enjoy,
Makenzi

UNEXPECTED

Truth

PROLOGUE

*W*here Phoenix lived people didn't dream of becoming doctors, lawyers, teachers or professional athletes. The people in her neighborhood dreamt about making it to the next day alive. Phoenix experienced a lot of bad times during her childhood years, and learned that even though there were areas in her life that needed improvement, it didn't mean she was a failure. Every day, Phoenix was told by men how beautiful she was, yet she knew she was not a movie star or model. She was just your average girl who grew up in the ghetto. Looks weren't everything. The outer surface told only a part of Phoenix's story. What lied beneath was what really mattered.

Today, Phoenix's life will change. The past few months had been rough for her, not knowing what her future held. She was unsure how to handle what had been happening in her life. This was the day that she had anxiously been dreading, her meeting at the Cuyahoga County Court at 9:00 a.m., court room 18-A. For court, Phoenix searched her closet for the perfect attire: a black Calvin Klein pant suit, a pink shirt and a pair of black BCBG pumps.

In the townhouse where she'd been residing for the last three years, Phoenix stepped out of the hot steaming shower, wrapped her wet hair in a towel turban, and slipped on her plush terrycloth bathrobe. She stood at the double-sink vanity, and wiped her hand across the mirror so she could peer at her reflection. She was mentally in pain. Butterflies grew in her stomach as she looked into the mirror, hoping to see the image of the person that was no longer inside her. Phoenix wanted to cry, but she knew she had a long road ahead of her and crying wouldn't change the situation. She crossed the line. The damage was done.

"I'm going to get over this hurdle in my life," Phoenix spoke to the image that looked her straight in her eyes with a worried expression on her face.

As Phoenix stood in the bathroom, she also thought about a meeting she had a few weeks ago with her attorney Anthony Lombardi.

a *a* *a*

"Tell me straight up, am I going to jail?" Phoenix had nervously asked as she glanced around Mr. Lombardi's office trying to avoid eye contact.

"Oh yeah, for sure," her lawyer had responded. "But for how long, that I don't know. That's up to the judge to decide. That's why it's very important that you make a great impression on the judge."

For a split second, the thought had entered into Phoenix's head—illegally leave the country and start a new life. She wasn't looking forward to the flavorless food, waking up early in the morning, and sitting around all day. She was not the type of person who enjoyed sitting around doing nothing. She was a mover and shaker. She knew if she left town or the country, the police and the bail bondsmen would be looking for her. Plus, she would constantly have to look over her shoulder while on the run. However, the main reason she could not and would not leave was because she just couldn't leave her friends and family behind, especially since they had put the collateral up on her bond.

Phoenix took a deep breath as she covered her face. Swallowing hard, she tried to hold back her tears, but inside, she was crying like a baby.

"Are you okay, Phoenix?" her attorney had asked. Phoenix did not respond; instead, she looked up at her attorney as tears started rolling down her face.

"No."

Phoenix shuffled out of her attorney's office with her head held down. She felt hopeless and helpless thinking about the information her attorney had just given her. As she sat in her car, she had screamed out loud "How did I let myself get in this shit?"

PHOENIX

1

$\mathcal{P}$hoenix "Fee" Brown was born on June 21, 1980, the first day of summer. She grew up on the east side of Cleveland, Ohio.

Phoenix, her brother Carnell, and sister Latasha lived with their mother Annette Hill in a three-bedroom house in the Glenville area, a predominantly black neighborhood. Growing up, their household was nothing like the Huxtables. In fact, they were more like the Beverly Hillbillies before they had money. The state of Ohio's welfare system raised the three of them. Every evening, their mother left the house and wouldn't return until the next morning, sometimes leaving Phoenix home alone long after Carnell and Tasha left for school.

It was the summer of 1986 when Phoenix first realized there was trouble in her household. Actually, it started the morning of her birthday. She was turning six. She remembered waking up with the biggest smile on her face…and no mother home, as usual. She jumped out of the bed she shared with Tasha. It wasn't long after that her mother came in the house with a plastic bag.

"Happy Birthday. How is my baby today?" Annette said, giving Phoenix the biggest hug she ever received.

Phoenix danced around the living room like she was one of the Jackson Five. "Yes, it's my birthday," Phoenix said, spinning around the room.

Annette ordered Phoenix to close her eyes because she had a surprise for her. Phoenix wondered if it was coming out of the bag that her mother brought in the house. She closed her eyes as tight as she could and waited for her mother's next command.

"Open your eyes," Annette said, bending down to hand Phoenix the one toy that she had asked for over and over all year long.

When Phoenix opened her eyes, her mother held a Cabbage Patch Kid. Well actually it was the fake version of the Cabbage Patch Kid, but in Phoenix's eyes, it was all the same.

Phoenix jumped up and down with excitement. "Thank you, Mama!" Phoenix repeated over and over.

"You're welcome, baby," Annette said before she left the room to go in her bedroom like she did every morning when she came in from being out all night.

By this time, Tasha had woken up and walked in the kitchen, hitting Phoenix in the head and pushing her around like she usually did. This day Phoenix didn't care what Tasha did because it was her birthday, and she received the best gift.

Tasha turned on the TV, so they both could watch the Saturday morning line-up of cartoons. Phoenix went into the kitchen and grabbed a bowl out of the cabinet for cereal to eat while she sat on the floor and watched cartoons.

Tasha was already in front of the TV, not taking her eyes off the Smurfs. "Last bowl," she shouted from the living room.

Phoenix paid her no attention; she grabbed the box of Captain O's from the bottom shelf. Mama never bought name brand cereal or anything else name brand, for that matter.

Annette would always tell them that she had to make her
money stretch, but each month they had less food in the house.

Phoenix opened the fridge and stared at three slices of
bologna, a week-old bowl of spaghetti, and a dark-brown
banana. There was no milk for Phoenix's cereal, so she had to
use what she always used when they were out of milk. Phoenix
filled her bowl with water and cereal and headed for the living
room to watch cartoons.

"It betta be some more cereal in the box, cuz you heard me
call last bowl," Tasha said, rolling her eyes and neck, grabbing
for Phoenix's bowl.

"Stop! I left you some," Phoenix whined, pushing her away.

Tasha headed for the kitchen, and Phoenix tried to hurry
up and eat her cereal because there was nothing left in the box.
Tasha stormed back into the living room. She kicked over the
bowl that was now sitting on the floor in front of Phoenix and
pushed her in the face.

"I said I had last bowl, so now none of us will eat." Tasha
crossed her arms over her chest like she was waiting for Phoenix
to say something.

Carnell and Tasha always called Phoenix a cry baby and
tattle-tell and today was no exception. Phoenix stood and
headed straight for their mother's room with Tasha right on
her heels.

"You talk too much, Fee, that's why no one wants to be your
friend," Tasha yelled, poking and pushing Phoenix in her back.

When Phoenix opened the door to her mother's room,
neither she nor Tasha expected to see what was going on behind
that door. Their mother sat on her bed with a thick rubber band
tied around her arm, sticking a needle in her arm while sweat

poured down her face. It was hot outside, but not hot enough for Annette to be sweating so profusely.

"Get the fuck out of my room," Annette tried to yell at her daughters, but her voice was weak. "Didn't I tell y'all black asses to knock before busting into my room? Close my door and go sit y'all fast asses in front of the damn TV, and let me have some time to myself." Annette could barely hold up her head.

After learning their mother was on drugs, life for Tasha, Carnell and Phoenix became pure hell. They barely had any food and had to beg and borrow food from neighbors. Annette went from staying out all night to sometimes not coming home for days; a few times she left for a whole week, looking for her next drug fix and when she would return home, her entire body had a foul smell, and she had track marks all over her arms. She also became very distant from her kids, sleeping all the time and keeping herself locked in her room.

After Kelvin—Phoenix's father—left their household, Annette's actions reflected how she really felt. She didn't care about anyone anymore, including her own kids. She didn't exactly tell Phoenix what happened between her and Kelvin, but when Kelvin first left and Phoenix questioned his disappearance, Annette told Phoenix that she once loved Kelvin very much and how he used to treat her like a queen, but over the years he changed, he wasn't the man she first met and loved, he became cold and selfish.

"Kelvin Brown, your father, is a no-good bastard" is what Annette would say after the love stories ran out, and Phoenix would shake her head in agreement because she was too young to understand what her mother's words meant.

Kelvin and his family were originally from Kansas. When he was a teenager, his family moved to Cleveland when his father was offered a better job opportunity. Kelvin was always into music and played in a local band.

Phoenix was four years old when Kelvin walked in the house one night, packed up his belongings, and told Annette right there on the spot he was leaving to go play with the band in Chicago. He kissed Phoenix on the forehead as she laid in her bed asleep. He grabbed his bags and walked out the door not even leaving a forwarding address, but he did leave a phone number for Phoenix to contact him.

Phoenix was hurt when Annette told her that Kelvin moved away. She wanted her daddy there, as he was the only person who would allow her to ride his back like a horse, tickle her until she couldn't laugh anymore and take her to the corner store with him when he would go to buy cigarettes, and a cold can of Colt 45. However, she especially loved that her father would always let her pick out a treat for herself like a bag of chips, a soda or a candy bar of her choice.

Even though Kelvin was not around, he made weekly calls to check on Phoenix, his only child. He had the same line with every call, "Hey little lady. Daddy just called to say hi." Those weekly calls kept a smile on Phoenix's face, and every week she anticipated receiving the next call. The calls lasted three years, and as time went on the love stories Annette once told Phoenix were replaced by verbal lashings every time she mentioned the name Kelvin Brown.

On top of her drug addiction and Kelvin leaving her alone to raise their children, Annette took her anger out on them. Annette was a great manipulator who knew how to get what she wanted when she wanted it. Her main concern was getting high and caring how the drug would make her feel. If it wasn't for Kelvin's sister Angie coming to the house, bringing food, and checking up on the kids, social services would have come and taken them away a long time ago; Annette was gone for days at a time.

When Phoenix was seven years old, she recalled one incident that stood out in her mind. The words and the tone of her mother's voice was unlike anything she had ever heard her mother say before.

"Mommy, I want to be a doctor when I grow up," Phoenix said, skipping around the house, watching the doctors on *General Hospital*.

"Fee, you ain't gon' be shit just like yo' daddy," Annette shouted, never taking her eyes off the television "Now sit yo' ass down and stop making all that damn noise, so I can finish watching TV."

Phoenix slowly sank to the floor; she was sad. Her mother's words brought doubt into her mind. Phoenix wasn't sure if her mother's harsh words were because she disliked Kelvin, her or both. Phoenix knew that things were different not just with her mother but with her father as well.

The weekly calls from her father became less frequent. As Phoenix sat on the floor pouting in silence after hearing, once again, her mother's verbal lashings, she mumbled to herself about how much she hated her mother for talking bad about her father and her father for not being there to prove her mother wrong.

"Ma, can I call my daddy?" Phoenix asked, because at that moment, she wanted her daddy, and because he wasn't physically there she picked the next option…a phone call.

"Yeah, but you better make it quick. I don't have no damn money to pay for a long distant call because his sorry ass ain't sending no money here."

Phoenix rushed to the phone, picked up the receiver and handed her mother the phone to dial the number. After Annette dialed the number she handed Phoenix the phone. Phoenix waited anxiously as the phone rang; it wasn't until the fourth ring that someone answered the phone.

"Hello," the male voice answered with a groggy voice, as if he were asleep.

"Hey Daddy, it's me Fee." Phoenix smiled through the phone. The sound of his voice always made her happy.

"Fee, you need to talk fast and say what you got to say because I'm busy," Kelvin responded, his tone bordering on rude.

"Daddy, are you going to come to my awards ceremony next week at school? I made the Merit Roll and Perfect Attendance."

"Fee, I have more important places I need to be, but I will try."

"Okay, I love you, Daddy," Phoenix said, enthusiastic, before ending the call. The only response she received was the sound of the line clicking. Kelvin hung up the phone without saying, "I love you" to his only child. This was a routine Kelvin had been doing for years, making false promises just to get Phoenix off the phone, but Phoenix was just too young to understand.

Phoenix was young and naïve in her mind; she thought her father would surprise her and show up. She told all of her friends and classmates that they could finally meet her father. The day of the awards ceremony, Phoenix waited anxiously in her chair with all the other third graders inside the packed gymnasium at Captain Arthur Roth Elementary School.

Shortly before the program began, Phoenix looked around the gym with a look of desperation on her face as she watched all the fathers and daughters showing their love toward one another. Kelvin Brown was nowhere to be seen; he never showed up to the awards ceremony neither did her mother Annette. However, unknown to Phoenix, Carnell was there sitting in the far back of the gym. He had skipped school to come watch his baby sister receive her awards.

After the ceremony, Phoenix spotted Carnell walking through the crowded gymnasium. She ran up and hugged him tightly, smiling as she handed him her awards. Even though Carnell was just a child himself, he was now the father figure Phoenix looked up to. However, in Phoenix's mind, he still could not replace the man she once called dad. On their way home, Carnell let Phoenix stop inside Dad and Son's store to pick out a bag full of candy, his reward to her for having such a great day at school.

Even at the young tender age of seven, Phoenix knew her mother's staying gone for days at a time, no food on the table, the landlord banging on the door at all hours for the rent money and the lights being shut off wasn't normal. Annette used the monthly money she received from selling her food stamps on drugs.

Phoenix watched Carnell, the oldest of the three siblings, and her father figure, hit the streets selling drugs at the age of thirteen. Someone had to support them because they couldn't count on Annette to be around. Phoenix stayed home alone very often; Tasha was always at one of her friend's house, and Carnell was barely home. It seemed like he only came home to sleep. He stopped going to school because the streets had officially taken over his life. He had a family to clothe and feed.

As the years passed, Phoenix put all the love she once had for her absentee father into her older brother Carnell, who had now stepped up and took on the role as the man of the house. Phoenix looked up to Carnell for everything. They would walk to the library, and Carnell would help her pick out books and when they came home, she would read to him. He would come home even if it was for an hour to make sure she ate, bathed and picked out her school clothes. He would walk her to school sometimes, and they even played checkers together. To her, he was her father, and she felt like he could never disappoint her. That's until the day she came home from school and witnessed him beating up their mother for stealing a few of his crack rocks. Carnell was punching his mother like he was fighting a man, beating her half to death while yelling in her face.

"No one disrespects me," Carnell shouted.

Annette broke away at one point and headed toward her bedroom. Carnell chased behind her as she threatened to call the police. She made it to her bedroom, and as she tried to close and lock her bedroom door, he kicked it open and started whaling on her, dragging her back downstairs.

While on the floor, Carnell punched, kicked and choked his mother, as blood oozed from her eye and nose. All Phoenix thought about was getting to Carnell and helping her mother.

Tasha leapt off the couch and jumped on Carnell, pulling on his right arm. Carnell used his left hand to knock Tasha to the floor. Carnell was only five feet tall and one hundred pounds, but it took both Tasha and Phoenix to pull him off their mother. Annette's right eye was completely closed. Carnell fucked up the right side of her face, and she was having trouble breathing. Carnell was walking around the house, talking about his finger was broken as he packed his bags to leave. Phoenix ran to her room, sat on her bed and cried, because another father was walking out of her life.

Kelvin returned when Phoenix was twelve years old. He was staying around the corner from Phoenix at his sister Angie's house. He just didn't want to show up at their door after all these years, so he sent his sister around the corner to bring his daughter to him.

Over the years, Phoenix had become angry with her father when he stopped calling and never came to visit. She hesitated leaving with Aunt Angie to go see Kelvin. Phoenix felt like he had a lot of nerve to showing up like everything was the same with them when he hadn't called, written or visited in five years.

When she walked in Aunt Angie's house, she looked into her father's face. It was as if she was looking at herself in the mirror—heart-shaped face, pointy chin and a sharp nose. Phoenix took after her mother in other ways; she was four feet in height, skinny and talkative; whereas, Kelvin stood a little over five-foot-nine with a slender build, and he was acting very shy. Kelvin looked dirty like he hadn't washed in a few days; he wore dark circles under his eyes looking like a tired, strung out, and washed up old man.

Kelvin eyed Phoenix, picking up on her ill feelings.

"Are you okay?" he asked, reaching out to hug Phoenix, but she stepped back.

"Where you been?" she asked, looking directly into his eyes.

"Phoenix, it will take me a while to explain that," Kelvin replied, breath smelling like cheap liquor. "But to make it simple, I left because I wasn't sure if you were my baby girl because your mama was a whore."

His words made Phoenix furious; she couldn't believe what this motherfucker just said. "What is it you want from me? For real, what you're saying right now I'm not trying to hear," Phoenix spoke with an increased attitude.

Kelvin smirked. "I just wanted to see you. It's been a long time, but I see you're stubborn just like your mama."

Rolling her eyes and poking out her lips, Phoenix backed up toward the door. This little get-to-know-you thing was over. "What do you expect? I haven't seen you in six years and you just pop up out of nowhere, get real."

"I didn't do right by you." Kelvin cracked a smile, not really caring that he was hurting Phoenix's feelings. "But I need you to know it wasn't your fault I left and never came back to check on you. That's my own weakness."

"You started a new life, but what about your old life? Don't even answer. Believe me, I never took it personal." Phoenix walked out the front door and slammed it behind her. Phoenix knew she had spoken a complete lie. She also knew this would be the last time she ever saw her so-called father.

Phoenix ran all the way home, crying. As soon as she walked in the house, she found her mother in the living room on the phone.

She watched her mother play shit off with Mrs. Leeland, the landlord's wife. Annette spoke to Mrs. Leeland like she was really concerned about what the lady was talking about, yet the entire time, Annette rolled her eyes.

Annette slammed down the phone, almost knocking the receiver off the hook.

"Nosey bitch," Annette yelled, placing her hands on her hips. "Who she think she is, calling here questioning me about money, asking did I give her husband the full amount of rent. I should have told her dumb ass 'damn right I paid my rent, part in cash and the rest in pussy.' Wouldn't that have been funny?" Annette slapped her leg and laughed. "I bet that would have stopped her from ever calling here again."

Annette looked at Phoenix, who had wandered in and sat on the floor.

"What's the matter with you, Fee?" Annette asked.

Phoenix told her mother what Kelvin had said. Annette hung on her daughter's every word, and when Phoenix finished telling her story, her mother explained to her that Kelvin had no choice but to leave.

"Fee, your father is a motherfucker. When I first told him I was pregnant with you, you know what he said? He said 'Nettie, you lying' then he drove me to the Free Clinic up there in East Cleveland and after the doctor told him I was pregnant, he yelled loud inside the clinic 'get an abortion'."

Speechless, Phoenix stood in front of her mother. Her stomach turned as she listened to her mother.

Annette took puffs from her cigarette in between her thoughts. "When we left the Free Clinic, Kelvin took me straight to the abortion clinic and when I refused to have the abortion, he made a scene at the clinic. Afterwards, he made me walk home.

"Once he finally accepted that I was keeping you, he drove me to the monthly doctor's appointment, but he would not bring me home. He made me walk home through rain, sleet and snow. He told me that he was doing it on purpose so that I might get hit by a car and lose you." Annette cracked a half smile and shook her head.

Tears formed in Phoenix's eyes as the story unfolded of her father's feelings toward her.

"How could a person not want their child?" Phoenix mumbled.

"Because he's selfish. I was tired of his bullshit. He was heavy on drugs, had lots of women, didn't want to work, and always borrowed money from me, taking the little money that I was to use to buy food to feed y'all."

Annette looked into Phoenix's face as she grabbed a Newport cigarette out the pack, lit it, and continued to talk. "He needs to stop pointing the finger at everyone and take responsibility for his actions." She took a long drag from her cigarette. "Sorry son of a bitch." Annette cursed out loud as she hurried up the stairs toward her bedroom, laughing while blowing out a huge smoke cloud.

Phoenix's blood was boiling. *I hate him*, she thought. *It's mean to say it, but it's true.*

MARCO

2

The summer of 1989, right before Marco was about to start the sixth grade, his mother and step-father Bill announced that they would be moving, and not just to a different county or school district, but to a completely different state. And not only that, but all of this was taking place in two weeks. That meant two weeks to say goodbye to all his friends, cousins and his favorite lady his grandmother, Grams.

Marco was upset; he pouted and whined the entire two weeks. "Ma, can't I just stay and live with Grams?" he pleaded, while watching his mother put clothes in the overstuffed suitcase that was lying on the floor.

"No, you're going and that's the end of this discussion. I don't want to hear another thing about it." His mother eyed him sideways as she rubbed her bulgy pregnant stomach that stuck out from underneath the shirt she wore.

"One of my friends said that the people in New Orleans do voodoo on you," Marco said.

His mother slightly chuckled as she swung her long black hair that hung over her shoulders. "Well maybe they will put you under a spell so you can stop asking the same questions."

Marco rolled his eyes; it was times like these that he wished he had a relationship with his father or even knew who his father was. When he brought up the subject or asked questions about his father, his mother would refuse to explain or tell him Bill was his father now. All Marco wanted to know was his name, what he looked like because everyone always told him how cute he looked with his round head, small ears, big eyes and wide smile. He knew he didn't look anything like his mother, so he figured he had to look like his father.

Marco respected his stepfather; he considered Bill to be his hero. Bill treated him like his own son. Marco considered his mother Marcy Sutton to be a great role model as well. She was a strong intelligent woman who spent many years as a single parent. She worked as a teller for Key Bank; before she married Bill, they never had a lot of money. They weren't rich or poor. Marco always assumed his mother felt guilty about raising her only child without a father because she would try to buy him material items to fill the void. It took a lot of adjustments for Marco and his mother going from a single-parent household to having a male figure constantly around.

Bill wanted Marco to be educated and exposed to the world, so they went to museums, fancy restaurants and sporting events, but Marco didn't consider it the same as having his own father in his life to show him how to be a man, tell him stories about his family and help him understand what it meant to be black.

Marco was desperate, so he tried something different. "Can I go live with my dad?"

His mother glanced up at him. "Didn't I tell you before to leave it alone? Now don't ask me again. No! The only people you will be living with are me and your father, Bill. Now get out of my face and go find something to do before you get in serious trouble."

Marco saw the look on her face and knew she wasn't playing. He grabbed his basketball and went outside.

I'm going to find a way to get back here, he thought as he bounced his ball up and down the driveway.

When everything was loaded into the car and the door to the moving truck was closed, Marco cried as he hugged his Grams who came over to say goodbye.

"You can come back to visit any time you want," Grams said, kissing Marco on the cheek.

Marco didn't want to leave Cleveland and move to New Orleans and attend a school with all those people he didn't know. The long drive gave him the opportunity to think about his new life; he planned to reinvent himself by finding friends that were more like him and less like the people in Woodmere that grew to become his friends over the last few years.

When his step-father pulled the tan Buick into the driveway, Marco looked out the window at his new home. It almost looked exactly the same as their house in Cleveland except it was brown with beige trimming, accented by white shutters and a newly constructed wooden front porch. The landscaping was new shrubs, and bushes neatly manicured and arranged in the lush green lawn.

Marco still remembered his first day of class. Everyone knew each other, which meant that they knew he was a newcomer.

"Good morning, class. We have a new student today," his teacher stated in a deep yet elderly voice. "Come on up and introduce yourself, young man."

"Me?" Marco pointed at himself as his teacher nodded.

Marco was nervous as he stood in the front of the class. "My name is Marco Brown," he said and then darted back to his seat. Being the new person made him the main topic of discussion among every group on the playground. How did he know? Because every time he passed a group of students, they stopped talking and just watched him.

"You new here, we've never seen you before? What's your name?" An extremely thin white boy with brown straight hair wearing a pair of too big blue jeans and a yellow t-shirt asked.

Marco looked up at him as he sat on the swing kicking rocks around. "My name is Marco. What's your name?"

"I'm AJ," the little boy turned and pointed to a skinny tall black boy standing next to him, "and this is Tyron. Where you from?" AJ and Marco smiled at each other.

"Cleveland," Marco bragged. He was embarrassed to admit that he actually lived on a street named Irving Park in Woodmere, a suburb of Cleveland. His cousins already teased him because he went to a predominantly white school, had a few white friends and a white stepfather. He wanted everyone to know he was proud to be black and not a wanna-be white boy whose mother married a white man with money.

AJ smiled as he covered his mouth. "Hey that's where Bone Thugs and Harmony from. Do you know them?"

"Nope, but they cool with my cousins," Marco lied.

"Why you come here? If I knew some celebrities I wouldn't ever move."

"My step-dad got a new job here. I wanted to stay in Cleveland and live with my Grams, but they wouldn't let me."

AJ, Marco and Tyron formed their own little crew, and the bond they had was strong. When you saw one, the other two were close behind. After six months of living in New Orleans, Marco didn't want to admit it, but he started to like his new home even though his heart missed his family in Cleveland.

PHOENIX
3

*T*he sound of the house phone ringing from downstairs woke Phoenix up out of her sleep. It was two o'clock on a muggy Wednesday morning.

What's going on? Phoenix thought. She couldn't imagine who could possibly be calling at this time of night.

Phoenix heard Tasha opening her bedroom door, yanking her door knob so hard it fell apart, falling onto the floor. Still half sleep, Tasha stomped down the stairs into the living room to answer the phone. It was pitch black in the house, but Tasha didn't flinch or even reach for the light. She had maneuvered around that house in the dark plenty of times and tonight was no different.

"It better be a damn emergency, calling my house at this time of night." Annette was cussing as usual from the inside of her bedroom. The walls were so thin that every word she yelled was heard loud and clear by Phoenix.

Mad that she had been woken from her sleep, Annette climbed out of her bed and opened her bedroom door.

"Tee, who is that on the phone?" Annette yelled to her oldest daughter before Tasha's foot even hit the last stair.

"I don't know," Tasha answered with an attitude.

Annette was getting more annoyed with each ring and was now standing at the top of the stairs.

"Tee, who the hell is on the phone?" Annette repeated with urgency after hearing Tasha talking.

Phoenix never left her room. She lay in her bed listening to the commotion happening outside her bedroom door. Phoenix saw a glow enter her room through the cracks of her door. Annette had turned on the hall light and was trying to listen to what Tasha was saying on the phone.

Tasha put the caller on hold and ran to the bottom of the stairs and started calling for her mother to come get the phone. Annette reached behind her bedroom door and grabbed her robe.

"Somebody better be dead to get me out of my bed," Annette mumbled as she ran down the stairs to get the phone. "Who is it?" Annette mouthed to Tasha.

Tasha frowned and shrugged her shoulders while answering her mother's question, "I dunno."

Annette rolled her eyes at Tasha. She was getting tired of Tasha walking around the house with an attitude all the time. "Give me the phone." Annette snatched the phone out of Tasha's hand. "Hello?" There was a slight pause. "Yes, this is his mother." After a few seconds, she added, "I'm on my way."

After she hung up the phone, Annette ran up the stairs to slip on some clothes. Half asleep, Phoenix heard her mother's trembling voice as she opened Phoenix's door.

"Fee, get up and get dressed. Carnell was admitted to the hospital."

"Ma, I don't want to go," Phoenix whined.

"Fee, I'm not in the mood for this now. Get up and get dressed," Annette commanded using a stern tone. She slipped on a gray shirt and a pair of jeans she grabbed off the floor in her room.

Phoenix finally mustered up some strength and moved around. She dragged her feet out of her bedroom and into the bathroom, where she sat on the toilet and fell asleep. Phoenix's eyes shot wide open after hearing a loud bang on the bathroom door, sounding like the person was about to break it down.

"Hurry up, Fee! Get outta there, I have to pee," Tasha hollered, banging on the door.

"Shut up, I'm coming," Phoenix responded as she jumped up, washed her face then unlocked the bathroom door and headed back to her room to get dressed.

"Y'all heffas hurry up," Annette yelled from the bottom of the stairs.

Annette didn't have a car and she didn't have any money for a taxi, so the three of them began the forty-minute walk to Huron Road Hospital in East Cleveland. Phoenix was extremely exhausted by the time they reached the hospital. When they walked inside the emergency room, Phoenix looked around and saw chaos everywhere. People were moving left and right trying to get out of the way or get past each other.

They were informed that Carnell was admitted for a drug overdose.

Phoenix was scared to death. They had been sitting in the waiting area for over an hour and no one had given them any information about Carnell.

"Ma, how much longer do we have to wait in here?" she asked.

"I don't know, but they need to hurry up and tell me something before I go the fuck off in here," Annette responded loudly as she stood and walked over to the nurse's station.

With a worried look, Phoenix stood and followed behind her mother.

"Do you have an update on my son Carnell Hill?" Annette asked the woman standing behind the counter.

"You think Carnell dead?" Phoenix whispered to Tasha.

Tasha replied with her arms crossed over her chest. "I hope not, that would be messed up."

"Hello, I'm Dr. Drake and I just finished up with Mr. Hill and you are?" The woman introduced herself, extending her hand to Annette.

"Annette Hill, his mother."

"Okay, Ms. Hill, Carnell had an obstruction in his airway, but—" Dr. Drake began to explain.

"I don't know what all that means. Is my son dead or alive?" Annette bluntly asked, cutting Dr. Drake off in mid-sentence.

"Carnell swallowed three balloons full of drugs, and one of the bags was stuck in his throat causing his air passage to become blocked. We had to pump his stomach to get the additional bags out, so yes he is alive," Dr. Drake explained while placing her hand on Annette's shoulder. "It's gonna be okay."

With an unconcerned tone, Annette asked, "Where is he now?"

Dr. Drake smiled as she instructed them on where Carnell's room was located. "Go straight down this hall and make a left. His room is at the far end of the hall right next to the emergency exit door. Room 1A."

The trio walked down an all-white hallway until they reached Carnell's room.

"Ugh," Phoenix said to herself as she entered the cold room. The room which Carnell was sharing with another man was run down. There was a television that only played four channels and two chairs that were side by side with stains on the cushion of the seats.

Looking at Carnell, Annette thought about her own drug habit and the many times she purchased drugs from her own son.

"Hey, baby." Annette smiled as she ran up and kissed Carnell on the forehead. "You scared me, boy. I almost had a heart attack." She grinned, and playfully smacked him on the arm. She was glad he was all right.

"Ma, stop, I'm in pain," Carnell mumbled under his breath.

Phoenix swallowed the developing lump in her throat as she kept her eyes on Carnell's face.

Carnell turned and noticed the worried expression on his sisters' faces. "Hey, Fee, Tash...what's up with you two?"

"Nothing," they answered in unison.

"I was scared you was really hurt." Phoenix said to Carnell.

"Ooh, my stomach." Carnell grabbed the side of his stomach.

"What happened, why you do that?" Tasha asked, turning up her face as she watched Carnell in pain.

"The police was sweeping the corner. I wasn't about to drop my work on the street. When I saw them pull up, I shoved the balloons down my mouth."

"Did it hurt, them pumping your stomach?" Phoenix asked him.

"Yeah a little, but you know me I can handle anything." Carnell slightly chuckled.

Phoenix had an outburst of tears. She loved Carnell; she could never stop loving him because he was her brother and the one person who took care of her. She disliked him at the same time for leaving her and Tasha alone at times to deal with their mother's drug habit.

"I'm going to the waiting room," Phoenix announced. The bad smell from the hospital room was making her feel sick to her stomach, and she thought the smell was penetrating her skin. As she turned to leave the room, she let out air through her nose, which sounded rough.

While sitting in the waiting room, Phoenix listened to a family that was sitting close to her talk about their twenty-two-year-old family member who was just admitted. He was suffering from multiple gun shot wounds to the head.

Phoenix was observing the entire scene that seemed unreal to her. A young woman sat in the corner chair, rocking back and forth, crying. "Why did this have to happen to him?" she kept repeating.

The mother was torn to pieces. "What am I going to do without my son?" She sobbed and fell into the arms of the lady next to her. The family was very emotional, crying and over-talking each other. Phoenix wondered if her mother would react this way if something happened to her.

Upon Carnell's release from the hospital, he moved back home. This made Phoenix very happy, having her brother back in the house because when he wasn't there she received no attention. Carnell took the empty space in the attic and slept on the old bunk bed that Phoenix and Tasha once shared. Carnell's main source of income came from selling drugs so he hit the pavement a few days after being released from the hospital. Plus Annette was still dipping into drugs, so besides feeding Phoenix and Tasha, Carnell had two additional mouths to feed—his son and daughter.

Phoenix really missed her brother. She missed the hugs he would give her, how he rubbed her head like a dog which always made her laugh, and him lecturing her about finishing her homework. She missed the stories he made up to keep her laughing, but most of all she missed him because in all her thirteen years living he was the only father figure she had in her life.

Phoenix was getting accustomed to the street life Carnell was living. He was building a name for himself around the neighborhood. Phoenix liked the attention she received when people in the neighborhood would refer to her as Nell's lil sis. She also liked the money Carnell gave her to go to the mall to buy clothes, shoes and occasionally to get her hair done at the salon.

"Here, take this," Carnell said, handing Phoenix ten twenty-dollar bills. "You and your lil friends go to the mall and get yourself something nice."

Phoenix's eyes got wide. "For real? Thanks Nell," she responded, wearing a huge grin.

Carnell smiled and grabbed the money out of her hand. "Sike," he joked.

"You play too much." Phoenix pouted playfully.

Carnell broke into laughter as he watched his baby sister's bottom lip protruding, as if she were upset. He handed her the money before he walked out the door.

Phoenix immediately called up her friends Shawna, Reese and Candy, so they could hang out for the day. They walked to Windermere Rapid station to catch the local bus to Severance Mall in Cleveland Heights. Phoenix spent every dollar Carnell had given her on a new pair of Adidas, a matching hat and seven outfits to match her new tennis shoes, and she brought lunch for herself and her friends.

When Phoenix returned home several hours later after being at the mall all day, shopping, being silly with her friends and flirting with the boys who roamed the mall, she was exhausted and wasn't in the mood for the altercation she was about to walk into with her mother.

"Ma, what are you doing?" Phoenix asked, catching her mother sneaking down the attic stairs from Carnell's room.

"Mind yo' business," Annette replied with a trace of anger in her voice while walking past Phoenix.

Phoenix knew if Carnell caught his mother sneaking down from the attic, he would go ballistic. After the beat down, he gave her years ago after the first time he accused her of stealing from him, Phoenix was scared he might end up killing her this time.

Phoenix loved her mother, but Annette was selfish, a loose woman who hung out on the street corners smoking crack. With Annette's heavy drug use, Phoenix didn't know if her mother had any emotions or love for anyone or anything but drugs.

"Do you even love us, Mama?" Phoenix asked with a bluntness that made Annette feel a chill to her bones.

Annette froze for a second, processing the question. "Fee, how dare you ask me that? Of course, I do." Phoenix's words hit Annette hard like a large boulder rock had been dropped on her head. Annette was at a loss of words.

Tears were now rolling down Phoenix's face. "Well I don't feel like you do. You walk around the house yelling for no reason. And if you really loved us you would stop using drugs."

"Mind yo' business and watch your mouth. Matter of fact, go sit yo' ass down."

"I hate living here." Phoenix almost choked on her own tears.

Infuriated, Annette slapped Phoenix in the face, trying to stop the pain from the question that Phoenix asked. "You're fourteen so you need to stay in a little girl's place."

Phoenix's lip bled from the powerful force of Annette's back swing across her face.

"I'm sorry! That was an accident," Annette said.

Phoenix was angry with her mother for reacting that way, but she forgave her. Tears continued to fall down Phoenix's face, but she didn't say a word. She was afraid if she spoke, if she made a sound, it would set her mother off once again. Phoenix feared her mother would stop talking and wouldn't answer the question she so desperately needed an answer to, so she kept silent. In the angry silence that followed, Phoenix stomped down the stairs into the living room to watch television.

Carnell walked through the front door and noticed Phoenix sitting on the couch with a blank stare. "You okay? You look like you were crying."

"I'm fine," Phoenix snapped at him unintentionally as she wiped her bloody lip with the sleeve of her shirt. Phoenix knew she had to lie to Carnell because if he knew what was really going on inside that house, with Annette stealing his drugs, she was certain someone would get seriously hurt, and her name was Annette.

MARCO

4

"Marco!" His mother's high-pitched voice traveled through the cracks underneath his bedroom door. "Get up! It's time for school!"

Marco inwardly groaned and threw the sheets off of him, swinging his feet over the side of the bed.

"I really…hate Mondays," he mumbled, wiping his face with his hand. The room swayed in front of him as he attempted to regain his balance. "I need to stop smoking weed." He laughed to himself as he glanced around his room. It really hadn't changed much in the last five years since they moved to New Orleans. The same green paint adorned his walls, the same posters hung on his walls, and the same shaky bookshelf he had since he was a kid still sat in the corner of the room.

A long mirror stood next to his closet, from which his clothes hung. After taking a shower, Marco slowly walked back to his room.

"What's up, lil man?" He playfully pushed his little brother who was standing in the hallway waiting to get into the bathroom.

Marco grabbed a pair of Levi's jeans and pulled them on, followed by his Cleveland Cavaliers jersey. He took the hoodie

36

that lay across the chair and roughly put his arms through it and zipped it up, completely hiding his jersey underneath it. Finally, he put on his matching Cavs hat to complete his outfit, grabbed his backpack off the floor, filled with his homework from the weekend, swung it over his shoulder and walked out of the room.

He opened the front door of his house, but stopped as his mom signaled for him to wait. "Have a good day, baby," his mother smiled as she kissed him on the cheek.

"I will," Marco replied before he slammed the front door. He walked to the back of his house, so he could take his usual route to school, which was to cut through the woods in the back of his house and from there he took the ten-minute walk down a residential street that led to his school.

As Marco walked into the school building and down the hallway, he looked around for the girls, a routine he did as he walked the same school hallway.

"AJ," Marco said, smiling after seeing his best friend walk up to his locker.

"What's up? How was your weekend?" AJ patted Marco on the back, grinning from ear to ear.

"It was okay, nothing really going on. You?" Marco glanced over his shoulder at his friend. They walked down the hall passing various classmates on their way to Tyron's locker.

"What's up, playboy?" Marco smiled as he approached Tyron's locker

Tyron returned the smile. "What's up?"

Marco was truly grateful to have friends like Tyron and AJ. Most people had been falling out with their old friends after about two years, but not them. The three of them had been best friends through thick and thin ever since the day they first met five years ago on the playground.

Another boring day at school, Marco thought as the bell rang dismissing him from Algebra class. When he reached his next class, he took a seat in the back of the room and slumped down in his seat. His mood instantly changed as he looked out the window in deep thought thinking about the scene he just witnessed in the hallway between his girlfriend Geneva and a classmate named Sean.

He didn't understand why Geneva would be passing or writing a note to Sean. He wondered what they had to talk about. He wanted to stop and find out what was going on between them, but he didn't have time because he couldn't be tardy for class any more this semester, or he would get detention and having a detention would cause trouble at home with his parents.

Marco could not erase from his mind how Geneva was flirting with Sean as she passed him the note and when she turned to walk away, she rolled her hips in the tight-fitting jeans she was wearing. She didn't notice Marco watching this entire scene of her smiling up in Sean's face, and now he was pissed.

"What's up?" AJ mouthed at Marco, noticing the instant change in his attitude. Marco shrugged. AJ frowned. "Geneva again?"

"Maybe..." Marco mouthed back, not in the mood to discuss what he'd just witnessed. He sat in his seat, glancing at the back of Sean's head. His concentration was broken as he glanced up at Mr. Franklin announcing to clear their desk for the pop quiz.

Still focused on the note passing between Geneva and Sean, the remainder of the school day was fairly uneventful for Marco.

After school, Marco, AJ and Tyron sat sprawled across Marco's living room watching TV and laughing. Marco was lying on one couch. AJ sat on the floor slouched against the front of the couch, his head tilted back, resting on the seat, and eyes closed. Tyron was stretched across the other sofa, flipping through a magazine. There was a knock on the front door with more force than usual. Marco looked out the window and watched as his girlfriend Geneva adjusted the straps on the red tank top she wore.

She smiled when Marco opened the door, but he rolled his eyes.

"Hey, papi," she said, but as soon as she walked into the living room and saw AJ and Tyron she sighed. She couldn't understand why a bunch of sixteen-year-old boys wanted to sit under each other every day all day.

AJ sat on the floor in complete silence. "What's up, Geneva, you talk to Sean lately?" he sarcastically asked.

She turned around and looked at AJ but ignored his question as she continued to hug Marco around his neck.

"Skank ho," Tyron said, not turning around to face Geneva who was now sitting on the couch next to Marco.

"What?" Geneva rolled her eyes. "You don't know me."

AJ chuckled and nodded in agreement with Tyron because they both heard from the horse's mouth what happened that previous Saturday night.

Marco looked around, confused. "What's going on?" he finally asked.

"Ask your girl, she's the one who's fucking everybody," Tyron said with an attitude. Neither he nor AJ cared for Geneva, but they tolerated her attitude and her mouth only because of their love for Marco.

"I heard today she fucked Sean over the weekend," AJ confessed.

Marco was completely caught off guard.

"I heard she just sucked his dick," Tyron bragged.

Marco turned around, furious, almost afraid to ask Geneva if it were true. He didn't care if she fucked Sean or sucked his dick. The fact was they were accusing her of cheating and he needed some answers.

"Papi, they are lying," Geneva said, trying to explain. She had sadness in her eyes, but no regret.

"They ain't lying, ho. I knew it was something going on after I saw you smiling all up in his face today at school," Marco yelled. He felt like he had something to prove because he was hurt. His ego had been bruised for the first time. He truly had feelings for someone and Geneva, the Puerto Rican Mami that he considered to be his girlfriend, was the one.

"No I wasn't." Geneva ran out of Marco's house crying.

AJ and Tyron left the house as well shortly after Geneva's drama-filled exit because they knew how Marco could be when he was upset and they weren't prepared for his rampage.

Marco lay on his bed and thought about the day he met Geneva in Science class. There was a couple of girls sitting in the row in front of him giggling about something, a boy at the end of his row was sleeping, and in the back of the room Marco, Sean, AJ and Mike sat at their desk laughing loudly and being annoying.

The rest of the class rushed in before the bell. A boy named Josh slid in and sat down next to Marco so that left the seat next to AJ empty. Just as the teacher started to talk, a girl with long black hair and a really pretty face came rushing into the room.

"You're late," Mr. Adams announced as he gestured to the empty seat next to AJ.

"Sorry, I couldn't open my locker," the girl replied.

"Don't let it happen again. There is an empty seat in the back."

As she looked over at the empty chair, she heard Marco and his friends laughing hysterically in the row next to her. She looked over at them and rolled her eyes.

"Now class, I'm leaving it up to you to pick your lab partners for today's lesson. Choose wisely," Mr. Adams spoke as he began writing on the board and everyone partnered up.

Geneva got nervous. She didn't know anyone, being the new student and all. How would she find a lab partner? It was just then that she felt a tap on her shoulder and when she turned around, she found Marco smiling at her.

"I'm Marco. Wanna be my lab partner?"

Geneva smiled. "Sure. I'm Geneva Santiago. Wait, do you know what you're doing?" she jokingly asked.

"Baby, I'm a genius," Marco flirted.

That was seven months ago and now Marco lay on his bed, watching TV, taking a deep breath and attempting to recover because at the age of fifteen, he had his first experience of a broken heart, and Geneva was the cause.

He lost his virginity to her. The day it happened, they both decided to skip school for the remainder of the day, and went to Marco's house because his parents weren't home. Geneva grabbed his hand and led him upstairs to his bedroom.

He had thought she was just as inexperienced as he, but when they reached his room, Geneva pushed Marco on the bed and sat on his lap. Marco took his hands and placed them on her breasts. He was a little scared because Geneva looked a bit uneasy; she assisted Marco with pulling down her pants.

"Papi, fuck me now!" she begged, rubbing her thighs. "Now, Papi, now!"

Marco nervously looked at her, not sure what to do next. He started sucking on her breast as he began pushing himself inside her. Geneva wrapped her warm pussy around his dick, causing her to shiver.

"Faster, Papi," Geneva begged as Marco pushed all the way up in her one last time before he exploded. She looked at Marco, smiling, tears rolling down her face. They both got dressed and Marco walked her home, kissed her on the cheek and smiled all the way back to his house.

"Marco, dinner's ready," his brother shouted from the hallway, snapping him out of deep thought.

When he sat down to have dinner with his mother, step-father and his younger brother, he kept his head down long after grace was said.

"Marco, how was school today?" Bill asked.

"I broke up with Geneva today," he confessed.

"What happened?" his mother asked in a concerned tone, looking up at her husband for guidance.

"She wasn't the one for me," Marco replied, giving her the don't-ask-because-I'm-not-going-to-tell look.

"Wow, doesn't she come from a good family? Isn't her father a doctor or something?" his mother continued to pry.

"Yeah, he—"

"Yes, not yeah," his mother cut him off.

"Yes, he is, but she still wasn't the one for me, no matter how great her family is," Marco answered defensively.

Marco turned his attention back toward his step-father. "I had a quiz in English class that I did well on and a Science test. I'm confident I got an A on that."

Bill smiled because he was proud of Marco and how dedicated he was with his school work. Marco sat at the table talking, but not really paying attention to the conversation he was having with his step-father. His thoughts were on Geneva. She hurt him, broke his heart, and disappointed him. He loved her, even though it was teenage love he stilled loved her, but he wasn't going back to her. His thoughts were focused on moving on with his life without Geneva.

Geneva tried to call Marco all week after the incident, but he wouldn't talk to her, and when he saw her at school he ignored her.

"Marco, I'm sorry, it was a mistake. I love only you," Geneva said sadly as she blocked him from walking away from his locker.

"You cheated. I don't date hoes," Marco bluntly said, pushing past her and walking away, leaving her standing there with her eyes filled with tears. Marco never considered himself to be a ladies' man, but he did know one thing for sure: he had a strong dislike for Puerto Rican women and vowed to never ever date one again.

PHOENIX

5

On yet another dreary October day, Phoenix walked down Woodside to the usual meeting place, Dad and Son's store on the corner of 128th and Woodside, where she met her friends at six-thirty in the morning, so they could walk to school together. Walking to school together was a routine the four friends had since childhood. As Phoenix approached her friends she overheard Shawna doing her usual whining.

"I don't want to go to school today," Shawna, whined as she, Candy and Phoenix stood outside the store waiting for their other friend Reese to get there so they could make the journey to Glenville High School.

"We can go to my house, nobody's there," Candy suggested. "We just have to be gone before two 'cause my daddy comes home around three o'clock."

"I'm sleepy," Reese added.

Phoenix was a junior in high school and a somewhat decent student. She thought school was boring, but she was scared to take a walk on the wild side because she knew the consequences of skipping and the possibility of getting caught. Phoenix witnessed it too many times as the loudspeaker came on in the classrooms and a list of names was read ordering students to, "Come to the principal's office immediately." Everyone's name who was called knew they were in trouble for one reason or another, so a few of them made scenes when they left the classroom.

"Let's go," Phoenix said as she began to walk toward the small alley leading to Candy's back door. The alley was always dark no matter what time of day, and the smell of piss clogged their noses.

Candy lived in a three-bedroom apartment on the corner of 131st and Brackland. From the outside, based on the appearance, the building looked like it was going to fall down at any time. There were broken bottles and trash lying on the ground, the fire escape ladder was hanging off the building, graffiti was written all over the brick building, and the screen doors were barely hanging on the hinges.

This is some nasty shit, Phoenix thought as she made her way inside Candy's apartment where she would spend the next five or six hours of her day laying around watching television, talking, laughing and having fun with her friends.

When Phoenix and her friends settled inside Candy's apartment, Shawna pulled out a pack of Kool cigarettes from her backpack and began to light it up. Phoenix watched her mother smoke every day, but she was still unfamiliar with the way to hold a cigarette and the inhaling and exhaling process. After a few puffs, Phoenix began choking and coughing really loud, causing large ashes to drop onto the floor.

"Fee, damn, be careful before you burn a hole in the carpet," Candy shouted, smacking Phoenix on the arm.

"Ouch! That hurt," Phoenix whined.

"Phoenix, will you walk to the store with me so I can buy some M&M's?" Shawna asked, changing the subject

"Okay, but we have to make it quick because my show is about to come on, *Family Feud.*" Phoenix smiled.

Shawna, Candy and Reese broke into laughter because they all knew how dedicated Phoenix was to that show.

As Phoenix and Shawna was walking out of the store, Phoenix heard a familiar voice calling her name.

She looked up and found herself face to face with Aunt Angie.

"Why are you not in school?" Angie asked with an attitude.

Phoenix looked at her aunt. "We didn't have school today. It's teacher's day."

"What's that?" Angie questioned, confused by Phoenix's answer. "They have teacher's day in high school?"

"Yes, I guess they do because we're off," Phoenix replied as she shrugged her shoulders at Angie's question. Phoenix began to laugh inwardly; she couldn't believe her aunt was actually buying her story.

"Okay, how's your mama doing?"

"She's fine," Phoenix responded with a fake smile as she turned around and continued to walk out of the store.

Back at the apartment, Phoenix sat down on the couch so she could watch the remainder of *Family Feud.* Her show was interrupted when she suddenly heard a loud commotion from outside. Phoenix jumped up off the couch and looked out the window to see what all the commotion was about.

"If I find out you touched my shit, I'm gon' bash yo' head in," a man's voice yelled to another man standing in the alley. "I swear I'll shoot yo' brains out."

"What's going on?" Reese asked Phoenix as she ran into the living room from the kitchen.

"I don't know," Phoenix answered. "Neither one of them will look up, so I can't see their faces."

Everybody pretty much knew everybody in the neighborhood, but from Phoenix's view neither one of the men looked familiar. The guy doing all the talking was short, stocky and muscular; he looked much older than the guy he was having words with. With the darkness in the alley, Phoenix couldn't see the other guy's face; she could only see the Cleveland Indians starter jacket and hat he was wearing.

The argument between the two men began to escalate, and Candy, Phoenix, Shawna and Reese were pushing each other out the way so they could each individually watch the drama that was unfolding in the alley.

"Man, Peanut, fuck you," the faceless man said as he began to walk past the unknown man now known as Peanut.

Peanut pulled a gun from the waist of his jeans and fired off three shots into the torso of the guy that was falling to the ground. A loud noise that sounded like fireworks was heard throughout the alley.

"Oh my God, y'all see this shit?" Phoenix blurted turning quickly to face her friends who were also watching from another window. As the guy fell to the ground, Phoenix felt her body go numb. Fear was written all over Phoenix's face. When the shots were fired, Candy, Reese and Shawna quickly moved from in front of the window, ducking down and crawling down the hallway toward the back of the apartment.

"Fee, what are you doing? Get down," Shawna yelled.

Phoenix didn't move. She stood in the window, shocked.

"*No!*" she screamed. It wasn't a normal scream. It was a chilling horrible sound like something from a horror movie. "Please say this is a dream," Phoenix spoke to herself as she grabbed her shoes. All she thought about was helping the stranger who was now lying on the ground helpless.

The shooter ran out the alley, jumping into a candy apple colored Regal and driving off. When Phoenix approached the alley, the sight in front of her was unbelievable. Carnell laid in a pool of blood, and Phoenix saw the entire thing.

There was blood all over the Cleveland Indians starter jacket he wore. Looking at Carnell lying on the ground, Phoenix felt like her spirit died at that moment, leaving her body cold.

"Please help me, please help me," he repeated.

Phoenix wasn't sure if Carnell knew he was bleeding as much as he was as she placed one hand on his stomach the other behind his head.

Phoenix grabbed Carnell in her arms as she sat on the ground and cried, rocking him. "Nell, it's me, Fee."

Carnell was moaning. "Fee, one side of my body is hot. It's hot, and one side of my body is cold. It's very cold." Carnell had no chance. His death came quick.

In the days after his death, Phoenix was filled with so much anger and loneliness. She was taken to the police station for questioning by a female officer the day of the shooting, so she could tell them what she saw while her friends had to write statements on everything that had happened.

Majority of Phoenix's relatives and family friends attended the funeral, even those Phoenix had never seen. People she had never met before greeted her with, "My, look how big you're getting" and "I'm terribly sorry."

Annette was torn to pieces as she, Tasha and Phoenix sat on the front row with devastated looks on their faces, all of them crying except Phoenix. She didn't want to show any emotion, so she tried to keep a smile on her face.

Annette sat in her chair, crying and shaking. "Is this my fault?" she asked Angie who was sitting next to her. "It's my fault, isn't it?"

Phoenix gritted her teeth. She hated that her mother decided to have a fix before services. She spent as much time scratching herself and acting up than she did crying over the loss of her son.

Angie looked up, wearing a black hat with a veil over it, her eyes red and puffy.

"Nettie, that isn't for me to answer. Whether or not I tell you it was your fault, it isn't going to bring him back. Carnell's gone."

The funeral was simple, nothing overdone, but filled with emotions. The pastor walked forward and faced the packed crowd inside Boyd's Funeral Home and began to speak.

"We are here today to celebrate the life of Carnell Hill. Leaving us so suddenly, he came into this world on February 12, 1977 and lived most of his life in the fast and furious streets of Cleveland."

In shock, Phoenix stared at the man talking. She couldn't believe he just said that. He didn't know her brother personally, so she didn't like the fact that he was judging him.

A few of Carnell's friends stood and told stories that made a few people chuckle and laugh. When the funeral was over, everyone left Boyd's wearing sad faces. Phoenix, Tasha and Annette all climbed into a black stretch limo that was waiting out front and drove to the cemetery.

BY THE TIME THEY MADE it home from the cemetery, Phoenix was through with her mother. She watched her mother dance around the house not too long after they stepped inside.

"Ma, stop you're embarrassing me," Phoenix said.

"This is my damn house and I can do what I want. I'm celebrating my baby's life," Annette responded, rolling her eyes. Phoenix left the situation alone; she knew her mother was hurting and was not mentally there.

The guilt of the broken relationship Annette had with Carnell was taking a toll on her. Phoenix overheard her mother sobbing continuously inside her bedroom late at night.

After her mother fussed and cussed at her, Phoenix hid in her room; she was tired of sitting around staring at the emptiness in her family's eyes.

"You okay?" Tasha asked as she walked in to check on Phoenix.

"Tasha, I'm going to miss him," Phoenix began to cry.

"Me too," Tasha replied.

The notion of human death was relatively unknown to Phoenix. At the age of sixteen, she was experiencing a feeling that she did not know how to handle. There was a piece of her family missing, and Phoenix was struggling to emotionally rebuild herself.

"How could he be dead?" Phoenix said as she and Tasha sat on the bed and cried together.

"Everything will be okay." Tasha tried to reassure Phoenix.

When Tasha left her room, Phoenix lay in her bed, crying, thinking about the relationship she had with her brother. Her heart was pounding; memories from eight months earlier sprang in her mind. Carnell had taken his mother, Phoenix and Tasha to dinner. They all had a great time laughing and joking during the entire meal.

There would be fights between the three siblings, which always resulted in Tasha and Phoenix jumping on Carnell, but Phoenix still loved her brother very much. Phoenix really wanted him to be at her graduation, cheering her on like he always did. Carnell always bragged about his sisters' accomplishments to his friends.

"Phoenix always gets good grades," Carnell would say. On the outside, this always embarrassed Phoenix, but on the inside she would smile at the great things her brother said about her. And now, there would be no more great things to be said from him.

MARCO
6

 $\mathcal{M}$ arco and AJ walked quickly to the basement before anyone would know they slipped into the house. Marco leaned against the washing machine, taking a long drag from the weed-filled black and mild cigar he rolled up inside of AJ's car. Marco loved weed ever since he started smoking in high school.

"This is some good shit. Where did you get this from?" Marco inquired, closing his eyes as he inhaled the smoke.

AJ laughed in agreeance with his friend. "Yeah, this shit is fresh. I got it from B."

Marco nodded. "This is all right." His eye widened when he heard footsteps walking down the stairs that led to the basement. "Fuck," he mumbled, taking one last hit of the blunt before dropping it on the ground and stomping on it with his foot. "Fan the air."

"What's going on?" His father spoke, looking Marco directly into his eyes

Oh God, here comes the bullshit, Marco thought for a moment before speaking. He didn't know what to expect because today was not the first time his father caught him smoking weed inside the house.

Mr. Sutton spoke with a hint of irritation in his voice and a look of disappointment on his face. "So you're going to just ruin your life?" he questioned. "AJ, please leave. I need to talk to my son alone."

"All right, Marco, hit me up later," AJ said, giving Marco hand grip as Marco nodded letting AJ know he would call him later.

"Son, I thought we had this discussion before and I told you the next time I caught you using drugs in my house it would be the last day you stayed here."

Marco didn't say anything. He stood frozen in place staring at the concrete floor inside the laundry room.

"You are almost twenty-one, so you're just going to ruin your life by doing drugs? Your mother and I put in a lot of effort in raising you, ensuring you had a good education and this is how you repay us, by disrespecting our household?"

Marco took a deep breath and rolled his shoulders. "I'm sorry," he replied, his glassy eyes pleading for his father to forgive him.

"Sorry! Do you know how many times you said sorry? You were sorry when you was stopped for the DUI. You were sorry for smoking weed in the bathroom. You were sorry when you failed two classes we had to pay for. Stop being sorry! You have until tonight to get out!" his father yelled as tears rolled down Marco's face.

"Fuck you! You ain't my real daddy," Marco spoke, his voice trembling uncontrollably.

Mr. Sutton clenched his fist in anger. "I may not be your biological father, but you are my son, and I will discipline you as long as you're living under my roof!"

Marco dropped his head because he was now feeling guilty for speaking to his father in such a horrible way.

"You gotta…" Mr. Sutton paused, his face turned pale as a ghost. "You gotta go, son. I can't have you doing this inside my house." Marco didn't answer. He stood in place, feeling his father's eyes on him. "Look at me, son." Marco looked up at his father. "Today. You got to go today."

Marco cleared his throat and spoke, wearing a fake smile. "Where am I supposed to go?"

"I don't know. You can go live on campus as long as you're still enrolled at Dillard. Me and your mother will pay for college or you can get a job and get your own apartment."

"All right, I will be out of your house by tonight," Marco angrily said, brushing past his father.

Marco walked into his room and packed all his clothing that would fit into the two garbage bags he grabbed out of the kitchen. He tried to clear his head from everything that was happening, but reality was sinking in that he had no place to go. He reached over to grab the phone sitting on his dresser and he began dialing numbers. The phone rang three times before anyone picked up.

"Hello," AJ mumbled half asleep.

"C-can I crash at your crib tonight?" Marco asked.

"Of course, you can. He really put you out?"

Marco took a deep long breath. "Yup."

"Damn, that's fucked up. You know you always got a place to stay here."

Marco tried to keep a smile on his face as he hauled the bags out to his truck, trying his best to show his father that he was all right with them putting him out of the house, but in reality he was scared and right now he felt like he wanted to punch a hole in someone's wall.

"Call me." Marco's brother Marcus hugged him. Marcus knew how much his older brother hated showing his emotions unless he was mad or unhappy. "I love you, big bro, take care and keep in touch, okay?"

"You act like I'm moving to another country," Marco jokingly replied, nodding as he looked over at his mother who was tearing up at the sight of him leaving. "I'll call you." Marco slammed the front door, leaving the house without saying goodbye to neither one of his parents.

BOURBON STREET WAS THE PLACE to be on Thursday nights. Everything and everyone was there—local residents, tourists, freaks, geeks, foreigners, dudes, chicks, men dressed as woman, woman dressed as men and the homeless.

Soul 2 Soul Thursdays at the House of Blues was where all the grown and sexy people came to see and be seen, so getting inside the club usually involved standing in a long line.

"How you doing?" Marco mouthed to a young woman waiting in line a couple of people behind him.

"Fine," she mouthed, blushing at the same time.

Marco had turned twenty-one a few days prior and because it was his birthday weekend, he was planning on celebrating hard, VIP style.

"Come on, y'all, let's go to the front of the line. My boy works security," AJ blurted out as he walked out of line after getting the okay from security to step up to the door.

As they walked in the club, Marco felt like all eyes were on him. Jay-Z was blasting through the speakers talking about "Do you need a balla? So you can shop and tear the mall up? Brag, tell your friends what I bought ya." People were grindin' each other on the dance floor.

"This bitch is packed," Marco whispered to Tyron as he scanned the room observing the model-type freaks throughout the club.

"What you drinking, birthday boy?" AJ asked, smiling at his friend.

"Yo boy drinking on Hennessy tonight," Marco answered, grinning with excitement. After being in the club for thirty minutes, Marco's attention was caught by a very attractive lady standing next to the bar. She was five-foot-eight and on the thicker side like Faith Evans. Her brown eyes and dark chocolate complexion accented the brown and blonde highlights in her hair.

Marco caught her glancing in his direction and the smile on his face grew when he noticed the teasing look on her face as she approached him.

"What's your friend's name?" she asked, biting down on her bottom lip as she focused her attention on the person standing behind Marco.

Marco tried to hide his disappointment as he looked over his right side to catch a glimpse of the person she was referring to. "Oh that's my boy Tyron," he replied as his eyes followed her figure while she leaned over the bar ordering her drink.

"He got a woman?" She waved a friendly hello at Tyron.

Marco secretly rolled his eyes with disgust. "You have to ask that man that question," he replied, a little annoyed and slightly jealous. He was tired of playing the wingman for his friends to pick up women.

"Well I think he is very sexy." She giggled out loud. Marco glanced at the woman who wasn't even paying him any attention. Her rude attitude didn't bother him because there were other female patron's inside the House of Blues who caught his attention. After dancing for several songs and a having a few shots of Hennessey in his system, Marco was officially drunk and was ready to leave the bar.

When they left the House of Blues, Marco, AJ, Tyron and Eugene, one of Marco's friends from college, sat inside the car in the parking lot for a few minutes, smoking the weed-filled black and mild that AJ pulled out of the glove compartment.

"I'm done with that," Marco said as he declined the blunt AJ was trying to pass to him.

Tyron looked at him like he was crazy, his eyes practically bloodshot. Tyron coughed, swallowing the smoke he just inhaled. "Get the fuck out of here! When you stop smoking? You smoke the most out of all of us."

AJ's car was quickly filling up with smoke, giving everyone inside contact highs. Marco shook his head and laughed. "Considering I did get put out of the house three weeks ago because of my weed smoking, I'm done."

Tyron laughed as he blew out a long stream of gray smoke. "I feel you. Have you talked to your mom?"

"Yeah, she called me on my birthday," Marco replied as he looked up at Tyron grinning stupidly.

"That's good shit. It sounds like they may be coming around to letting you come back home," Tyron replied as Marco looked at him from the corner of his eye, not saying a word.

There was silence in the car as AJ drove to drop off Tyron and Eugene. Marco sat in the backseat, thinking about calling his parents to apologize, his shoulder pressed against the window. Even though he was still angry and hurt that his parents put him out of the house, he knew he had to be the one to apologize and ask them if he could come back home because even though he loved having freedom, he was tired of sleeping wrapped up in a sheet and a blanket on the floor in AJ's room.

The next morning Marco called his mother at her job. He knew if he called her there she wouldn't be able to fuss at him like she would if he was face-to-face with her.

"Health and Human Services, Mrs. Sutton speaking."

Marco's eyes widened with excitement at the sound of his mother's voice. "Ma, can I come back home?" he blurted.

"How are you?" his mother questioned. "Do you feel like you've learned your lesson?"

"I'm good." Marco struggled with what to say next; his words were caught in his throat. "Seriously, Ma. I have nowhere else to go!"

"Are you sleeping in your truck?" his mother asked, trying to keep her voice low as if she didn't want her co-workers to overhear her conversation.

"Not that it matters at this point, but no, I'm sleeping on the floor in AJ's room," Marco mumbled. "Are you still mad at me, Ma?"

"Not mad, but disappointed."

"Ma, I swear I'm sorry. I even stopped smoking. I want to come home. I don't want to live here or on campus in the fall. I miss you guys."

"Baby, bring your butt home. I will tell your father I said it was okay."

"Thank you. I love you, Ma," Marco said, jumping up and down with excitement. They both hung up the phone and Marco moved as fast as he could around AJ's bedroom packing all he could in three garbage bags.

Thirty minutes later he was in his truck headed home.

PHOENIX
7

"Carnell....Car-nell..." Phoenix opened her eyes and looked around the room, trying to figure out where she was. She was tangled up in her sweat-soaked sheets. A deep sense of loss remained inside of Phoenix from missing Carnell. During the past year and a half since Carnell's death, Phoenix was occasionally haunted as she would see images of the incident in her mind; she would also hear in her head the words the shooter spoke to Carnell, "I swear I'll shoot yo' brains out."

She couldn't erase the image of Carnell lying on the ground. She'd seen him die a hundred times in her dreams, shot in a drug deal gone wrong. She hated hearing the sound of Carnell's begging voice.

Phoenix inhaled and exhaled heavily for a couple of minutes before she got out of her bed.

"Tasha, you sleep?" Phoenix asked in a flat, lifeless voice as she entered Tasha's room in the middle of the night.

Tasha groaned in annoyance as she opened her eyes, turned on her back and stared at the ceiling.

"Are you crying?" Tasha asked. Tasha waited for Phoenix to make some kind of comment; instead, all she got was silence.

Phoenix weakly responded, "No," but her choked-up voice betrayed her words. "Tasha, I keep replaying what happened in my mind over and over. I will never forget the shooter's voice for as long as I live." Phoenix never told anyone including the police that when the shooter ran away from the scene she saw the make, model and color of the car he was driving.

"In time you will forget what his voice sounds like and you will be able to move on."

"I doubt it," Phoenix replied. "I doubt it."

Carnell's death was a huge blow to Phoenix and her family. Being nearly halfway through her high school years was one of the worst times such a tragedy could occur. Phoenix was in a state of shock. Carnell meant the world to her, the only father figure she'd known; they had a bond like no other. She was his little princess. Phoenix felt her brother's death was unfair.

Phoenix was on an emotional roller coaster. Her body was physically attending school, but her mind was shut off. Phoenix stopped participating in the class discussions; she became distant and would sit in her seat staring off into space. On the weekends she would stay in bed and sleep. The simplest things made her upset. Phoenix's daily routine consisted of going to school and coming home and getting in the bed.

After Phoenix graduated from Glenville High School, she decided to attend Cleveland State University, majoring in Business. Having extra money from her Pell grants and financial aid allowed Phoenix to enhance her appearance as she spent her money on the latest BEBE, Coogi, Baby Phat or whatever else brand name designer she decided to wear.

Phoenix was mingling with more people around campus. She was enjoying the attention, especially from the athletes who were passing her their phone numbers in class or constantly requesting her presence at parties or to just hang out in their dorm rooms.

During Spring Break of her freshman year, Phoenix went to Daytona Beach with Shawna and Candy. Shawna booked them at some motel on the beach located right on the boardwalk. They packed up Candy's Camry and headed down to Florida. They drove all night until they crossed over the Florida state line. They were excited the entire fifteen hours it took to drive from Cleveland to Daytona Beach. Daytona Beach was full of black people from everywhere.

When they pulled up to the motel, they were not impressed. It was a two-story motel that looked like it was rarely cleaned. The motel's doors were made out of metal and shook when they walked past them.

"I'm sorry," Shawna said as she shook her head and chuckled. Neither one of them really cared what the motel looked like. As long as they had a place to lay their heads for the next three days, they were fine. The next three days were going to be full of drinking, parties and men.

On their first night in Daytona, they arrived at a party at Ocean Deck Beach Club. There was a line that stretched around the building. After being in line for nearly twenty minutes, Candy started making conversation with a group of guys in line ahead of them.

"Are you all from here?" Candy asked.

"Naw, we're from Louisiana," one of the guys responded with a strong southern accent. He continued to tell them they attended Dillard University and were staying at the Radisson off the beach.

Candy, Phoenix and Shawna entered the club without being carded, even though they were all under the legal drinking age.

"Slow down, girl, you gon' hurt yourself with all those tequila shots you're drinking," a sexy brown-skinned guy said as he walked up to the table where Phoenix and her girls were standing. He grinned as he watched Phoenix take down shot after shot of Tequila.

"I'm a big girl. I can handle anything," Phoenix said, smiling in return, rocking her hips back and forth to the beat of the music.

"This bitch is jumping," the stranger stated to Phoenix while looking around the crowded party.

"Yeah, this party is the shiiit," Phoenix shouted while throwing her hands in the air. "Nigga, I'm the colonel of the muthafuckin tank. Y'all after big thangs, we after big bank," Phoenix yelled out as she rapped along with Master P.

"What's your name, lil lady?" he asked her.

"Phoenix, but everyone calls me Fee," she yelled in his ear over the extremely loud music.

"Nice to meet you, Fee, with yo' sexy ass. I'm Marco." He grinned at her. "Are you old enough to be drinking that?" Marco jokingly asked.

"Of course, I am." Phoenix laughed knowing she was lying. "But you don't look old enough yet…kid. Why you not drinking? How the hell you even get in this place?" Phoenix was so drunk she was falling onto the table and hanging on to Marco's arm at the same time.

"No kids here, I'm twenty-one and legal," Marco replied as if he was bragging.

"I would have said no more than twenty, but you look like you're eighteen," Phoenix jokingly replied

Marco leaned in and whispered in her ear. "If you don't mind, how about you and me go somewhere else, so I can get to know you a lil more?"

"That's cool. First let me tell my girls I'm leaving." Phoenix wiped away the liquor dripping from her mouth. She turned to her left and whispered in Candy's ear "Don't wait up for me." She winked at her friend and walked out the door with Marco.

The effect of the liquor was making Phoenix feel good, but helpless at the same time. As they walked toward the parking lot, Marco grabbed Phoenix from behind, and she could feel the hardness from his dick poking her ass. She wanted him inside her really bad; her pussy was soaking wet.

When they approached Marco's truck and climbed in the back seat, Phoenix reached down and grabbed his hands, pulling them up to her voluptuous breasts. He teased her nipples with his fingers and then started kissing them; she started kissing him back on the right side of his neck, pulling Marco close to her as she rotated her body against his. Phoenix was becoming very aggressive; she unbuckled Marco's shorts and pulled them down. Marco could tell Phoenix was drunk because she was talking very loud, laughing and giggling at nothing particular.

Phoenix was single and enjoying her college life. Sex to her had always been an expression of lust and love for a person she was in a relationship with, until now.

"Oh my God," she yelled, "It's huge." Phoenix continued to talk as she wrapped her fingers around his dick, trying her best to hold it with one hand as she stroked it up and down.

When Marco lifted Phoenix's skirt, to his surprise, she wasn't wearing any panties. He knew it was time to get down to business. She opened her legs, and her feet were now in the air bouncing up and down with Marco's every stroke as he pumped hard and pressed deep into her walls.

Marco moaned when he came inside of Phoenix. She soaked the seat of the truck as both of their juices poured out of her. After they finished, both Phoenix and Marco put on their clothes. They got out of the truck and walked slowly back toward the bar, holding hands. When they approached the door they stood by the door, talking for about ten minutes.

"Breakfast, lunch, dinner?" Marco asked still holding Phoenix's hand.

"Can I get a rain check? This is a girl's only weekend?" Phoenix giggled like a little kid.

"I'm going to hold you to that?" Marco smirked, crossing his arms comfortably over his chest.

Phoenix smiled flashing her perfect smile as she grabbed a napkin off the nearby table, pulled a pen out of her purse and wrote her cell phone number on a napkin.

"I hope to hear from you soon," Phoenix mouthed to him as handed him the napkin before walking away to join her friends for more drinks.

The following day, the trio hung out on the main strip where they were guaranteed to find action everywhere. Phoenix, Candy and Shawna stood around watching a parade of half-naked women walk by. Everywhere they turned; girls were posing for pictures, and guys held video cameras, taping everything. Girls were dancing on the beach and on top of the hoods of cars. Shawna flirted with every guy who walked by.

There were all sorts of events hosted at the hotels on the beach from Luke's Freak Show to wet t-shirt contests; there was even The Best Beer Bottle Sucker contest that Candy participated in and won second place.

AS THE THREESOME DROVE BACK to Cleveland from their three-day vacation, they laughed as they shared their Daytona Beach stories.

"This shit is bangin'," Phoenix said while turning up Jay-Z's "Money, Cash, Hoes." Candy and Shawna nodded their heads in agreement.

"Hey, did I tell y'all I fucked Ron last week?" Candy spoke with excitement

"I already fucked him a few months ago, and he likes to do some freak-eee shit," Shawna chimed in as she turned toward the back seat watching Candy flick ashes out the window from the Newport cigarette she was smoking. Shawna was waiting on Candy to respond to her comment, looking for some type of reaction, but Candy ignored her and continued to smoke her cigarette.

"Damn, Shawna, who haven't you fuck?" Phoenix laughed as she shook her head with disappointment at Shawna and glancing through the rearview mirror, watching the look of disgust on Candy's face.

"I can't help it. I love niggas with money." Shawna smiled flashing Phoenix the finger.

Phoenix rolled her eyes at Shawna's gesture; then her mind wandered off to the mystery man she had sex with in the back of his truck. She still hadn't told her friends what happened when she and Marco left the club. Even though her friends wouldn't judge her actions, she still felt embarrassed and stupid for having sex with a guy she didn't know, within an hour of meeting him.

Right now, Phoenix's mind was all over the place. She wasn't sure if he would call like he promised? Did he think she was a ho? Would she ever see him again? Would he run and tell all his friends what happened? Then she stopped in mid-thought smiling because she really didn't care if Marco did or didn't think she was a ho or called because to her Marco was only a one-night stand.

PHOENIX

8

"C'mon, these bitches are crazy." Phoenix was laughing her head off as she watched the Maury show. "They tested nine men, and they still don't know who the daddy is." Phoenix continued to giggle to herself, and then she started feeling really, really sick. She felt vomit working its way up to her throat and within seconds, it gushed from her mouth and all over the floor.

Phoenix jumped off the couch, knocking over the cereal bowl, and ran into the kitchen. She stood with one hand on the kitchen counter and the other hand on her stomach as if she might throw up again.

"Damn, was the milk spoiled?" Phoenix asked as she reached for the refrigerator door, opening it and grabbing the milk to check the date. "This shit is good for another week." She started swallowing hard as her stomach gurgled.

"What the fuck did I eat?" Phoenix spoke aloud as she mentally replayed the night before. "I hadn't eaten shit yesterday since like noon."

Twenty minutes had passed and she hadn't felt sick, so she jumped in the shower, so she could get dressed and rush to her English class to turn in her final assignment. While in the shower and after already spending five minutes bent over the kitchen sink, Phoenix felt like she had to throw up again, so she got out of the shower and bent her head over the toilet but nothing came out.

She quickly went to her phone and dialed. At the sound of the beep, she left a message. "Professor Ewen, this is Phoenix Brown. I'm in your eleven o'clock Tuesday and Thursday 101 classes. I'm calling because I think I have some type of stomach virus, and I won't be able to make it to class on time to turn in my assignment. I will make sure you have it by five today. If I'm not feeling better, I will have someone drop it off at your office. Have a great day. If you need to call me back, my number is 851-7229."

She made her next call.

"Hello?"

"Come to my house," Phoenix said, panicking.

Candy was silent for a moment. "Fee, are you okay?"

"Um, Candy..." Phoenix hesitated "Can you bring a pregnancy test?"

There was a brief moment of silence again. "Yeah, I'm on my way," Candy finally answered.

Phoenix didn't want to be pregnant, especially by whom she knew the father was. She didn't want to have anything to do with him.

"Thanks," Phoenix said before they hung up the phone.

It took Candy ten minutes to get to Phoenix's house. Annette wasn't home, so Candy didn't have to hide the pregnancy test.

"Here you go." Candy handed Phoenix the pregnancy test. "I had an extra one at home."

Both Candy and Phoenix had worried looks on their faces

as Phoenix went into the bathroom and peed on the stick. It took three minutes for Phoenix to get the results.

"Damn!" Phoenix screamed.

Candy ran into the bathroom. "Fee, you okay?"

Phoenix was speechless. She held up the stick.

"Damn," Candy said, looking at the stick "Who you pregnant by?"

"I think that guy I fucked on Spring Break because I haven't fucked any new dudes yet," Phoenix answered, embarrassed.

"Who?" Candy was confused.

"I never told y'all about it because it didn't matter at the time, but do you remember the guy I left the bar with in Daytona?"

"Oh, shit! I forgot all about him."

"Well, I fucked him in the back of his truck."

"Damn, Fee, he didn't use a condom?"

"Girl, I was so fucked up, I don't know what the fuck he used. All I remember is we fucked in his truck." Tears began to fall from her eyes.

"Have you talked to him?"

"Yeah a couple of times, but nothing serious. I was attracted to him at the time, but I can't say I like him. Hell I can't even remember what he looks like."

"Are you going to call and tell him?"

"Yeah. I will, but I'm still getting over the shock myself." The thought of being pregnant scared Phoenix. She didn't know what to do or say at that point except, "I'm having a baby," and rub her stomach, with a slight smile.

The next day, Phoenix sat on her bed and stared at the phone, her hands sweating because she was nervous about the dilemma she was now faced with. Phoenix began shaking as she dialed his phone number. Questions raced through her mind. *What am I going to say? What's going to happen?*

When Marco answered the phone, Phoenix's heart sank and her stomach began to flip as she considered backing out and not telling him. The conversation started out slowly as they took the time to catch up on what each other had been doing since the last time they spoke.

"Marco, I'm pregnant," Phoenix blurted out.

"What?" he asked, shocked.

"I'm pregnant, but I can't be that far along," she said quietly.

"I'm..." Marco stopped talking, unsure of his answer "Fee, I'm not ready to be a father, plus we live so far away. Don't you think this is unfair to you, me and the baby?"

"I guess...okay then," Phoenix responded, biting her lip as her eyes watered. All she wanted to do was get off the phone and cry because she felt a tear building up momentum and beginning to slide down her face.

Marco spoke in a calm tone. "I will Western Union you the money for the abortion later this week." He paused and before he could speak another word, Phoenix slammed the phone on him.

Marco called back and Phoenix let the call go to voicemail. "So you just gon' hang up on me when I was talking? Sorry things happened the way they did. I wish you the best in all that you do. Again, I will send that to you by the end of the week. Take care," Marco said, ending his message.

Phoenix fumed with anger and sadness at the same time as she listened to Marco's message. She wasn't sure what she would do, but she knew she had to make a decision—and soon.

"PLANNED PARENTHOOD, PLEASE HOLD."

Phoenix was starting to get annoyed because she had been holding on the phone for five minutes. It had already taken her a week to get up the nerve to call and make the appointment.

"Thank you for calling Planned Parenthood, how can I help you?"

Finally, someone picks up the phone. They keep you on hold long enough to make you want to change your mind, Phoenix thought. "I would like to make an appointment."

"Okay, what type of appointment would you like to make?" the woman asked.

Phoenix paused; she felt embarrassed that she had to make this type of phone call.

"Sweetie, you still there?"

Phoenix whispered in the phone. "I need to have an abortion."

"Can you talk because I have some questions to ask you?"

"Yes, I can talk," Phoenix responded, twisting the top on the bottle of hot pink nail polish she was using to paint her nails.

"Okay, have you taken a pregnancy test and received positive results?"

"Yes."

"When was the start date of your full last complete period?"

"March 18th."

"That puts you at about seven close to eight weeks. Are you a student, military or receive Medicaid?"

"Yes student, no and no," Phoenix answered, shaking her head, forgetting she was on the phone.

The lady slightly chuckled. "We have two options. The local which is $265 if you're fewer than twelve weeks, then we have the twilight which is $330 under twelve weeks. With twilight you will experience a dizzy feeling so someone will have to drive you home."

"Okay."

"You have to listen to a recording. It explains the procedure. I'm about to transfer you. Don't hang up. After the recording ends, someone will come back on the line and set up your appointment."

The three minutes it took for the recording to finish seemed like a lifetime to Phoenix because she wanted everything to be done and over with.

"When would you like to schedule?" a different lady picked up and asked.

With a heavy sigh, Phoenix answered, "I guess as soon as possible."

"We only schedule Monday through Thursday. Which day would you like to come?"

Phoenix leaned over and grabbed the yellow piece of paper off the dresser. "I guess Monday." She searched for a pen to write down the date and time.

"I have a ten o'clock or ten-thirty available."

"Ten-thirty."

"Name?"

"Do I have to give my real name?" Phoenix felt a little reluctant with giving her name fearing someone would find out her business.

Phoenix could hear the woman smirking while she talked. "Yes, because you have to show some form of ID when you come."

"Okay, Phoenix Brown," she mumbled.

"I have you down for Monday at ten-thirty. Do you have any questions?"

"Nope."

"Have a good day."

After Phoenix hung up the phone she immediately felt like a little girl lost. She suddenly felt an overwhelming sense of fear and sadness inside her. She curled herself up in a ball and cried herself to sleep.

SHAWNA DROVE PHOENIX TO THE abortion clinic. Phoenix signed in, scribbling her name on the line and then filled out the paperwork the receptionist handed her. After Phoenix finished the paperwork, she took a seat and looked around the room at the young girls waiting to have their name called. Phoenix wanted to tell the girls not to do it, but who was she to tell someone not to have an abortion since she was there for the same reason?

"Don't worry, girl, it doesn't hurt. I've been here three times already," Shawna said, trying to console her friend after she noticed her shivering and rubbing her arms.

Phoenix crossed her arms, lifted her eyebrow, and looked at Shawna with disbelief. She could not believe her friend had the nerve to be bragging about being at the abortion clinic three times. Phoenix began thinking this was probably one of the biggest mistakes of her life, a decision she would have to live with. As she sat waiting for her name to be called, she looked to her left out the window and watched the people out front with their signs. She felt so numb, and in a daze that it didn't even click with her that the people were outside protesting what she was here doing.

"Phoenix Brown," a woman called out; her voice caused a chill to ripple up Phoenix's spine.

Phoenix blankly looked at Shawna as she stood to walk behind the door. Shawna smiled at her. Phoenix went into a room and spoke with the nurse, going over again the procedure then they ran lab tests. Phoenix got undressed and was given an exam and some pain medicine. She then waited for the doctor to enter the room. She lay on the table as the male doctor slid a cold metal instrument inside her. He then inserted a tube and began to suck away at her insides.

As Phoenix waited for her ordeal to end, her thoughts were focused on what it would be like to have a baby. *What will he or she look like? Would I be a good mother or turn out to have many flaws like my mother? What would my baby grow up to be? How would this change my life?* Phoenix felt uncomfortable and was cramping really bad. Though the entire procedure took about twenty minutes, it felt like hours to her.

When the procedure was completed, Phoenix was taken into the recovery room. There, she found some girls sleeping, a few crying and some that didn't show any emotion at all. Phoenix stayed in the recovery room for about an hour. As Phoenix prepared to leave, the nurse handed her a white piece of paper that had the after-care instructions, the dos and don'ts. The receptionist scheduled Phoenix a follow-up appointment for two weeks, and then she was released to leave.

"Finally, this shit is over," Phoenix said as she walked toward Shawna. As they walked out the building, she began to cry.

"Are you okay?" Shawna wrapped her arms around Phoenix to give her a hug.

"Yeah," Phoenix lied with a slight smile. Actually she felt empty inside and just wanted to be alone.

"Wait here while I get the car." Shawna ran to the parking lot. When she pulled up to the door, Phoenix slowly got into the car.

"I really appreciate you doing this for me, Shawna," Phoenix said giving a fake smile.

"Girl, shit happens and you know I will do anything for you." Shawna returned the smile as she pulled out the parking lot.

Shawna's words brought a real smile to Phoenix's face. Over the years they had been through a lot of shit and they never turned their backs on each other and that meant a lot to Phoenix to know she had some true ride or die friends.

MARCO
9

Marco hadn't realized it until now, but the actress that played Jody's baby mama in the movie *Baby Boy* reminded him of Phoenix. The first time he watched the movie, he never noticed it, but now as he watched the BET movie of the night, he thought that Taraji and Phoenix could pass for twins separated at birth. The only difference was Phoenix's hair was shorter than the chin length bob Taraji wore. He couldn't get Phoenix off his mind. He needed to talk to her for some unknown reason.

I only knew her for a day. Why do I feel this way? Is it because she carried my child at one time? No, that can't be it. What is it? Then it crossed his mind that he will be in Cleveland in a few weeks for business, and also the fact that he and Phoenix had unfinished business to discuss. He couldn't pretend she had an abortion no matter how long ago it was. She was the first and only woman who carried his seed. Marco felt if he didn't owe Phoenix anything he did owe her an explanation for asking her to get an abortion.

He sighed as he punched the numbers into the phone. He wasn't sure if the number was the same after two years, but he took the chance of calling anyway.

"Hello?" The woman answered, the sleep was thick in her voice.

"Hello, how are you?" Marco's heart was pounding and his palms were sweating profusely. He didn't know what to expect from this call or even explain his reasoning for calling.

"Who is this?" Phoenix sounded uninterested as she slightly raised her voice.

Marco didn't answer her question. Instead he replied, "You don't remember me, Ms. Phoenix?"

They both laughed.

"No, or I wouldn't have asked," she said, her voice was pure sarcasm. "So we know each other?"

"You could say that," he replied, smiling through the phone.

Laughing lightly, Phoenix replied, "Whoever this is, you need to stop playing games or you will be talking to the dial tone."

"It's Marco, Phoenix. How are you doing?"

"Wow, it's been a very long time, stranger. How are you?"

"I'm doing great. I can't complain, life is good for a brother right now. Is this a bad time for you, do I need to call you later?"

"I can talk, so…to what do I owe the pleasure of you calling my phone today?" They both laughed uncontrollably at Phoenix's question.

"Umm." Marco sighed, his forehead was starting to sweat.

"Umm, is not an answer," Phoenix said sarcastically.

"Phoenix, I'm sorry I didn't call sooner. I felt really guilty about how things went down, but I had to suggest what I did because the timing wasn't right. I thought about you a few times over the years." Marco stuttered through his apology, as this was the moment of truth.

Phoenix released a sigh of frustration. "Sorry for what? That it took you two years to call and check up on me? I dealt with and fixed the situation. There really isn't a reason to call with a sorry now. Don't you think it's a little too late? I'm not mad, but what's up? You still haven't told me the reason for this call?"

He laughed at the sarcastic tone in Phoenix's voice, but he also felt a little relieved that she didn't hang up the phone on him, even though she would have the right to without an explanation. He swallowed hard. "I just don't want you to hate me, but I'm coming to Cleveland for a business meeting next week and to visit some of my family there."

"Oh okay, where do you work? You have family here, where do they live?"

"I work for Nestle in Houston, but I have a meeting at our office in Solon. Is that close to where you live? I was born in Cleveland, but I have family that lives off Kinsman, Shaker Heights and my grandmother lives on Throckley in Cleveland."

"That's right you did tell me you were from Cleveland, but it's been so long since I talked to you, I forgot. But Solon is about thirty or forty minutes from my house."

"Do you think it would be possible for me to take you out to dinner, maybe you can show me around town?"

"How long will you be in town?"

"Four days."

"Okay, we can have dinner. Now the showing you around town may be a different story." Phoenix laughed.

"What's so funny?"

"Nothing. So what do you do for Nestle?"

"I'm an accountant."

"Wow an accountant. Do you like working there?" Phoenix was impressed with what she was hearing so far from Marco.

Marco chuckled. "Yeah, it's a decent company to work for. Did you finish school?"

"I wish. I graduate next year." Phoenix smiled so hard Marco could feel her smile through the phone.

"What's your major?"

"Business Management with a minor in Marketing."

Slowly as the sun came up, they both began to fall asleep on the phone. They spent hours catching up, getting to know each other. Phoenix felt so comfortable talking to him that she told Marco how her brother Carnell's death hurt her really bad, something she never shared with any other boyfriend.

"Okay I have to go," she said eventually. "I have class in a few hours."

"Aww, the conversation was just getting good." Marco laughed. "Can we pick this up again later?"

There was a pause then Phoenix began to speak. "We'll talk again soon."

"Sure, okay," Marco mumbled not satisfied with the answer. "Have a wonderful day, beautiful."

"You do the same," Phoenix replied before hanging up the phone.

Marco felt good after his long conversation with Phoenix. All day at work he replayed their phone conversation. For some reason his mind kept going to a place where Phoenix was his and he was hers. He shook his head to clear his mind, at one point he dreaded going to the conference in Cleveland, but now he looked forward to the visit more than ever.

PHOENIX
10

"*A*re you excited?" Reese asked as she sat on the edge of Phoenix's bed watching her put on her makeup.

"Excited about what?" Phoenix tried to sound as if she was calm, but she was nervous and excited at the same time.

"You haven't seen this man in two years, and when you did see him it was for what…a day. Then he calls out of the blue after two years and asks you on a date. What if you don't like him? What if he's a killer? Where are you going?" Reese's voice held concern.

Phoenix smiled and looked at Reese for being so overprotective. "We're meeting at Capers, inside the Marriott on Chagrin. I figure that's in the middle for both of us, plus he doesn't know his way around."

"Make sure you leave me his full name and number in case his ass tries something."

WHEN PHOENIX STEPPED THROUGH the door, she anxiously looked around the busy restaurant and spotted the red polo shirt that Marco told her to look for when she arrived.

He was sitting in the corner booth drinking a Heineken. She smiled as she approached the table and was greeted with the same excited smile from Marco as he stood to give her a hug.

Damn he smells good, Phoenix thought. She looked him up and down. He seemed taller than she remembered and now wore a goatee and a low-cut Caesar. Phoenix thought he was very attractive and wouldn't have ever taken him as the corporate type.

"Ms. Phoenix. Wow, you haven't changed a bit. You're still beautiful as ever."

Phoenix blushed and playfully hit Marco on the arm before sliding into the booth. "Well thank you, sir." She was starting to become embarrassed. She couldn't stop showing her teeth; she'd been constantly smiling since she walked through the door. Phoenix looked over the menu, but her mind was preoccupied thinking about Marco's reason for calling after two years of no communication.

"So what are you ordering?" Marco spoke, breaking the silence at the table.

Phoenix looked up at him and smiled once again. She looked closely at the menu and sighed. "I'm not sure, but I'm hungry. I haven't eaten much all day. I wanted to make sure I spent all of your money and I've been walking around with an empty stomach." Phoenix smile but Marco looked at her with a raised eyebrow. "I'm just kidding." She laughed, tickled at herself.

"I was about to say, you better hope they have a dollar menu." They both laughed. Marco made Phoenix laugh so hard tears welled in her eyes.

Phoenix wiped her eyes and glanced around the restaurant. "It's crowded in here for a weeknight."

Marco shrugged his shoulders and grinned. "I wouldn't know if this was crowded or normal."

The waiter took their orders. Phoenix ordered fried shrimp with a glass of wine, and Marco ordered Shrimp Alfredo. When their food arrived, they were so into their conversation that they didn't notice the waiter walk up with their plates.

"So not to be nosey or anything, but what does your man think about you being out to dinner with me?"

"He's here spying on us." Phoenix laughed

"For real, where is he? Tell him to come out so I can meet him," Marco sarcastically replied, looking around the restaurant.

"You would hit the floor if he walked over here." Phoenix nervously played with her napkin.

"No I wouldn't. I would be like, what's up, man? You got a good woman."

Phoenix grabbed her cell phone, pretending to make a call. "Bay, come over. He would like to meet you."

"Okay, I see you're a class clown." Marco nodded.

"Even if I did have a man, it wouldn't matter. I mean, we're just friends, right? Well, *becoming* friends." Phoenix found it almost impossible to look away from Marco.

"Right." Marco answered. Phoenix could hear the disappointment in his voice.

From what she had witnessed so far, Marco seemed to be one of the few men she met that wasn't full of himself. Phoenix was impressed at how easy it was to talk to him; they had a lot in common. She felt like she had a real connection with him.

"I had a boyfriend, but we broke up a year ago." Phoenix shrugged, like it was no big deal. "Since then I've gone on a few dates here and there."

By the time they finished eating, drinking, laughing and talking, two hours had passed as they walked out the restaurant. Marco faced Phoenix, and extended his hand to her.

"Oh, sorry, I was just in deep thought," Phoenix mumbled with a smile, but she was really admiring how handsome Marco was.

As they walked out the building hand-in-hand, they passed an elderly couple also walking hand-in-hand. They smiled, and both Marco and Phoenix returned the gesture.

"It feels good out here," Phoenix said, commenting on the warm but breezy seventy-five-degree weather.

"This is perfect compared to how hot it gets both in New Orleans and Houston."

"You're lucky you don't get snow. It gets so cold your ass literally freezes up and it takes hours to thaw out." Phoenix laughed uncontrollably as she fell into Marco's arms.

"I wouldn't mind living here," Marco slid in, trying to get a reaction from Phoenix.

"Cleveland!" She laughed, taking his words as him making fun of where she lived. "Stop joking on my city."

"No, I'm dead serious, it would be a change in scenery plus I can keep my eye on you." Marco laughed but he wasn't joking. He put his arm on her shoulder and whispered in her ear. "I wouldn't mind taking care of you." He eyed Phoenix's five-foot-seven, one-hundred-seventy-pound frame. Marco loved thick women and Phoenix was the perfect match for him.

"What do you mean by that?" Phoenix asked playfully.

"I'm just letting you know that if you were my woman, I would take real good care of you." Marco kissed Phoenix's cheek. "Believe me when I say from what I've observed you're worth it." He hugged Phoenix.

Phoenix blushed as her stomach did a nervous flip. "Umm, very impressive, Mr.," she paused. "What's your last name?"

"Brown."

Phoenix smiled at Marco. "Stop playing. Brown is your last name?" She laughed.

"Yes, Brown is my last name. What's so funny?" Marco smirked.

"Because my last name is Brown. I hope we're not related. That would be a shame." She continued to laugh.

Marco played with her hand. "It sure would be a shame because if we got married and we are related, we would be like those people in the hills of West Virginia." They both laughed as Marco walked Phoenix to her car and opened the door.

"Can we do this again tomorrow?"

Phoenix nodded yes before closing her door. Marco leaned down and kissed her on the lips before walking away to his rental car.

The next day Marco called Phoenix at five o'clock in the evening, reminding her of their date that night, as if she had forgotten already. Phoenix smiled as she talked to Marco, thinking about how much she enjoyed their date the previous day. It was better than she had expected.

"Pack a bag for tonight, I'll be there in an hour" Marco spoke through the phone.

"Pack a bag for what?" Phoenix curiously asked

"Because I want you to stay with me tonight," Marco answered

"Ummm, let me think about that," Phoenix paused, pretending like she was thinking about her answer. "Alright but don't think you getting any." She laughed

"I'll see you in a few." Marco replied as they ended the call.

Phoenix ran up to her room and began stuffing some clothes into her duffle bag, before Marco arrived for their date. Marco arrived at Phoenix's house in an hour flat, he hooked the horn and she walked out the house carrying her duffle bag. Marco jumped out the car ran to Phoenix's side of the car like he did on their first date, he helped her inside the car and then he shut the car door.

"You're such a gentleman." Phoenix mentioned between her smiles

Marco looked at Phoenix smiled "Only because I have a beautiful lady with me."

The car ride wasn't as awkward as Phoenix expected it to be, considering she knew in a few hours she would be having sex with Marco, why else would he ask her to pack a bag to spend the night with him.

Marco drove them back to the Marriott hotel in Beachwood, this time they skipped past Capers and walked to the area where the elevators were located, they both got on and Marco pushed the button that took them to the fourth floor. When they arrived at room 408 Marco opened the door and tears immediately formed in Phoenix's eyes from the sight.

Marco had the room decorated with pink and red balloons, in the middle of the bed was a huge heart made from Hershey kisses candy, the Jacuzzi was filled with pink and red rose petals, two wine glasses sat on the night stand and in the mini fridge was a bottle of chilled Moet. That night for the first time in two years they made love to each other, Phoenix felt like her and Marco had a fiery connection, a feeling she had never experienced with any other guy.

Three Months Later

"FLOWERS AGAIN? THAT COUNTRY BOY must really like you." Annette laughed as she picked up the note attached to the flowers; they were Pink Roses this time—and read it: *You brighten my day---Marco.* Phoenix looked at her mother's face and there was a dreamy look in her eyes. Despite her sunken eyes, skeletal body frame and the tired look she wore on her face, Phoenix knew she was once a beautiful woman.

Phoenix replied over her shoulder, "Oh, he likes me." She walked upstairs to her bedroom to call Marco.

"That's my girl." Annette laughed, shaking her head until Phoenix was out of her sight.

"Thanks for the flowers." Phoenix smiled flopping down on her bed, her cell phone in one hand and her pillow with her other hand. She had strong feelings for Marco because he always treated her differently than any of her previous boyfriends, in a good way.

"You're welcome, baby, how was your day?"

"Fine, I'm just tired. My body feels like I've been hit with a bat." Phoenix rolled her shoulders back

"What have you been doing?"

"Nothing, I'm not getting enough sleep, I have so much homework."

"Six more months and my baby will be a Cleveland State graduate."

"Ugg that time can't come fast enough."

Marco chased Phoenix strong long distance and she loved every minute of it.

He wined and dined Phoenix in the most romantic ways. They did almost everything together from flying on weekend getaway trips to New York City, Vegas and the Bahamas to having flowers delivered to her house, sending cards just because and sending her to spa treatments. Marco had her on cloud nine; he would call just to see how she was doing or how her day was and after three months from when they reconnected, they both agreed to attempt having a long distance relationship.

When they first agreed on the long distance relationship, Phoenix was almost positive that it wouldn't last because of the living distance between them. But as time went on and they began traveling together and Marco would make more frequent visits to Cleveland. Phoenix began to feel that no one in the world had a stronger bond than her and Marco they had a very strong partnership and they trusted each other with their lives. The shared both good and bad memories with each other, life experiences they had never shared with anyone else. Phoenix knew that Marco was the man for her because he accepted her for who she was flaws and all.

MARCO
11

"I'm so proud of you." Marco smiled at Phoenix from across the table; the way his full lips stretched out over his sparkling white teeth made Phoenix's heart flutter.

"Thank you." She smiled backed. "I was so nervous. It felt like forever before they called my name. I almost cried because the people around me were hugging and crying it was getting sad."

"Cry baby." Marco jokingly grinned. "It was a lot of people graduating, the building was packed."

"All I know is when they said Phoenix Brown, I heard you shouting my name really loud." Phoenix burst into laughter.

"I wanted everyone in the building to know how proud I was that my baby was a college graduate," Marco said, smiling from ear to ear. After Phoenix's graduation, they left the Wolstein Center and drove a few blocks downtown to Mallororca restaurant to celebrate.

Marco knew the relationship he had with Phoenix was stable and steady; it was more than just a physical connection with her. He felt like she was a part of him, they talked about everything, they rarely had a dull conversation, they opened up

88

to each other about everything from his father not being a part of his life, his past relationships, her mother being on drugs, her father not being in her life and even about her brother's death.

Phoenix could change his whole mood with a few positive words; she always looked for the good in every situation. She was the one who made his heart skip a beat. Marco loved her. He could never stay mad at Phoenix. All she had to do was smile and he would instantly forgive her.

"I bought you a gift, but I didn't wrap it." Marco winked at her with a smile as he reached in his pocket and pulled out a box. He knew the moment was right because Phoenix was surrounded by people who loved her. He flipped the box opened and inside was a ring. "Phoenix, you're beautiful, funny, you're perfect for me." Marco spoke, his voice holding a hint of nervousness. "Will you marry me?" A million happy thoughts raced in his mind as he grabbed Phoenix's hand.

Phoenix looked at Marco, smiling. "Yes! Of course I will," she replied, jumping up and down with excitement as people in the restaurant watched the joyous occasion. "Ladies, I'm about to be Marco's wife." Phoenix bragged to her mother, sister and grandmother as she waved her finger in the air.

TWO MONTHS AFTER MARCO PROPOSED marriage to Phoenix, he transferred his position from the Houston office to the Nestle office in Solon.

"Do you like it?" Marco questioned, speaking about the huge brick duplex townhouse they were in the process of renting from a private owner. They chose to move to Euclid because the drive was thirty minutes from Marco's job and fifteen minutes from Phoenix's new job at Progressive Insurance in Mayfield.

Phoenix nodded. "Yes, I love it." She had never lived with another person besides her mother and sister, so sharing space with someone besides them was new to her. Neither one of them had much furniture. Marco sold the majority of all his furniture before he moved to Cleveland because he knew Phoenix would want all new furniture. Right now they had the basics, but it was going to take more than a few pieces of furniture before the townhouse became their home.

"DAMN, WHERE AM I?" MARCO jumped up out of his sleep after hearing the television in the bedroom playing. For a second he panicked until he looked over at Phoenix who was cuddled up next to him sleeping; they had been living together for seven months now and at times he still wasn't used to living with anyone. He sat up in the bed and looked at the clothes piled in a basket that was sitting at the foot of the bed. He got out of the bed and walked to the closet and after opening the door he laughed to himself because he eyed his side of the closet and then over at Phoenix's side. His side had has his shirts hanging neatly in a row, organized by color and style. Shoes and pants were lined up in the same manner.

"Neat freak." Phoenix sat up in the bed laughing as she noticed Marco staring at her side of the closet. Marco personally hated when things were a mess, but he wouldn't trade Phoenix for anything. If getting married to the most beautiful woman in the world meant him tripping over a bunch of her shoes or him cleaning up the dishes from her latest cooking experience, then it was all well worth it.

"I'll show you a freak." He began tickling Phoenix as she walked toward him.

She let out a laugh as she wrapped her arms tightly around Marco as he stood looking in the closet. "Don't start nothing you can't finish."

"You are in troooouuuuble, little lady. It's Friday so I can be late for work." Marco turned around, navigating Phoenix back toward the bed.

THERE WAS NO SOUND IN the townhouse except for the television, no smell of dinner being made, no sound from his best friend's voice. Today was just another boring day for him. Phoenix was out with her friends, busy planning the wedding, a routine she had been doing on Saturdays for the last few months. It was a strange feeling for him being home alone; besides two of his co-workers he didn't have many people he hung out with on the weekends. His cousins were into clubbing all the time, something he just wasn't into anymore since he moved to Cleveland, so whenever they would call he would send the call straight to voicemail.

After surfing the web for about an hour he became bored so he turned off the computer and went back to watching television. He tore his eyes from the screen and squeezed them shut, after being sleep for a couple of hours he woke up and wiped his eyes, clearing his blurry vision. He looked at the clock it read seven-thirty Phoenix had been gone since ten o'clock that morning and it was already getting dark out side.

"Hey baby, when you coming home?" Marco asked, sounding sad.

Phoenix giggled through the phone. "I'm sorry, baby. I'm on my way home now. It's just been crazy planning this wedding. Trying to decide what I want."

"Yeah I understand, but I know everything will be perfect because I know my baby, and she won't settle for nothing but the best." Marco stared at the television, his mind taking in all of the vibrant pixels and flashing lights as he watched Sports Center. He yawned and stretched his arms over his head, letting them drop back down onto the back of the sofa.

"I'm excited. I can't wait until we get married, but the day will be here before we know it," Phoenix spoke with excitement. "Are you excited?"

"Of course," Marco replied.

"Well I'm pulling up now," Phoenix said before they ended the call.

Marco had thought he'd be nervous about getting married after hearing horror stories from his co-workers and a few friends but he wasn't. He was just as excited to get married as Phoenix, he looked forward to the next chapter in his life with Phoenix, which was suppose to be grand.

MONDAY MORNING, MARCO SAT AT his desk inside his office and prepared for another mindless work day. He loved working for Nestle. He didn't have a dead end job, he just didn't feel challenged anymore, so he began getting bored with his job and this rolled over into his personal life. He wanted excitement, adventure because right now all he did was go to work, go home, spend time with Phoenix and on occasion he would go out for drinks with a few of his co-workers.

Right at that moment he needed a good laugh. Ever since Phoenix put him onto Craigslist when she was on there looking for deals for the wedding and he accidentally clicked on the personal ads, he found himself logging in every day to get a good morning laughing off the postings.

Marco laughed hysterically. "Hell naw, 'lonely man seeks fun filled woman to take away his loneliness.' This shit is wild. Their asking to have their dicks sucked, threesomes, and they offer money just to be with a fine woman. This shit is ridiculous." As he skimmed through the ads, his attention was caught by one particular posting: *Nubian Queen looking for Prince Charming to have some fun.* Marco thought the female in the picture was beautiful; her eyebrows were thick and perfectly shaped, her nose was tiny, full lips, jet black curly hair, light eyes and a perfectly round ass. There was something else about her that caught his eye, a small mole above her right upper lip that looked very sexy on her. Marco didn't see any harm in responding.

"Its email, they don't know me," he whispered. He typed a short reply: *Hey mami you looking good.* He felt his heart physically throb as he typed every single word and clicked send.

Marco was in deep thought when he heard a voice whisper into his office. "We have a quick meeting in the conference room." He put on a fake smile, grabbed his notepad and pen, and walked down the hallway toward the conference room. He grabbed the chair closest to the door so he could make a fast exit once the meeting was over because he was completely uninterested in what his manager had to say.

After his morning meeting, Marco returned to his computer and grinned when he noticed he had a response that read: *Hey Daddy what's good? Send a pic.* After Marco received a reply he wasn't sure what to do. *This chick can be a stalker, a man or a killer.* He laughed out loud, but he took a chance and typed another reply: *I'm good mami. After seeing that round ass of yours I have*

no choice but to be good. Marco grinned as he hit send for the second time, but this time he attached a picture of himself after he photo shopped Phoenix out of the picture.

He spent the remainder of that afternoon emailing back and forth, conversing with his new friend. She was boosting his ego, and it made him feel good. He looked at his watch and realized it was five o'clock…time to go home.

"First time in a while that I can say work was fun," he said, chuckling. He logged off the computer, reluctant to do so, and figured he would never chat with the woman again.

But he was wrong. They emailed a couple of times a week for the first three weeks, just general conversation, mainly harmless flirting with each other. The flirting started to increase and Marco went from logging into his email at work to at home in the morning and late at night. Before Marco knew it, he gave her his cell phone number because he wanted to hear her voice.

MARCO WATCHED AS PHOENIX SORTED through her wedding binder, ensuring she had everything she needed. She was on her way to Detroit to spend the day with Christian, the wife of Marco's cousin Kory. When they met a few months ago at his grandmother's seventy-fifth birthday party, they connected. Phoenix would always talk about Christian, saying things like "Christian said she would do my hair and makeup for the wedding" or "Christian offered to help me pick out my wedding dress." He was happy Phoenix was building a friendship and connection with his family because his family meant the world to him.

An hour after Phoenix drove off headed to Detroit, Marco picked up his cell phone and noticed he had a voicemail message. He called his voicemail and listened to his message. Holding his phone to his ear, he heard a voice that sent a shiver through his body. *Hey Daddy, give me a call and stop playing games, you know how much I want you.*

Marco smiled as he returned the phone call. "How you doing, pretty lady?"

There was a soft giggle from the person on the other line. "I would feel much better if you were here inside of me."

Marco wanted to see how serious she was, so he pushed the bar and began having phone sex with her. "Baby, take your free hand and run it across your breasts and down along your stomach and stroke the insides of your thighs for me." After a few minutes, Marco heard the moans escape her lips as she rubbed the inside of her thighs. Marco's dick began to throb from her moans.

"Mmm…Baby…I'm not going to last long with this phone sex. I need you here inside of me," Lourdes pleaded. Marco wanted to see her, so he wrote down her address and walked out his door.

HE WAS NERVOUS WHEN HE finally arrived at her place and nervously knocked on the door; he heard faint footsteps nearing the door and the sound of kids screaming from inside. The door clicked opened.

"Hey boo." She smiled.

"What's up, Lourdes?" Marco's eyes widened as he walked in the house, keeping his eye on the figure in front of him. She looked nothing like the picture she sent him a few weeks back. In the picture she looked like a model dressed to kill in a short mini dress that complemented her curvy figure and a pair of stiletto heels to complete the outfit. In person even though she was still pretty, she looked used up and tired.

Lourdes sat down on the couch but not before Marco eyed her ass jiggle in the tight black Capri pants she was wearing. She sat down and began flipping through the magazine that was sitting on the couch beside her.

"Y'all take yo' asses in your room with all that damn noise," she screamed at the three little kids that were running around the house playing tag. At one point Lourdes must have felt Marco staring at her because she looked up, her eyes locked with his for a second before she smirked and went back to reading. "So did you find my apartment okay?" She asked, keeping her eyes in the magazine.

Marco took a deep breath. It had already taken him three weeks to finally come visit Lourdes and now he was nervous about being there and the twitch of his dick confirmed his nervousness. "Yeah, your directions were perfect."

"So you finally came to visit me." She smiled grabbing the blunt off the table and began smoking it. "You a fine chocolate thang, just how I like 'em." She widened her smile.

"So you like to smoke?" Marco asked with a curious expression.

"Yup, it makes me calm but more importantly it makes me horny." Lourdes raised her eyebrows. "You smoke?"

"I smoke a little every now and then," he replied and after two hits Lourdes passed the blunt to him and he began to inhale.

Marco winked at her. "Good information."

"Trust me. It will be worth the ride," Lourdes flirted.

For the next hour and a half both Lourdes and Marco sat on the couch watching TV, talking and smoking. They kissed and smoked more weed and then kissed again. From that conversation Marco found out Lourdes' full name, that she went to Cuyahoga Community College and that she just got out of a bad relationship with a guy that was twelve years younger than her and who is also the father of her youngest child.

Lourdes got up from her spot on the couch and sat next to Marco. She nervously ran one hand through her hair, never breaking eye contact with Marco. "Do you mind if we go somewhere more private?" she asked and Marco shook his head, letting her know it was fine. Lourdes grabbed his hand and led him out of the living room and into a small room with nothing in it but a full size bed, a dresser and a chair from her dining room set that sat in the corner.

Marco felt his mouth drop when they entered the bedroom; he tried to avoid looking around, but the room was a mess, a real mess. Dirty clothes were scattered all over the floor, cups with juice was on the floor by the bed, and there was a plate with food left on sitting on edge of the dresser.

He sat on the bed and waited for Lourdes to finish in the bathroom and check on her kids. When she finally opened the bedroom door, she was wearing nothing but a pink bra and panties. Lourdes licked her lips when she noticed Marco staring. She unsnapped her bra and slowly slid the straps off her shoulders, revealing a pair of B cup breasts that would easily fill his hands.

Lourdes walked over to the bed and rested her knees on either side of his thighs; she sat on his lap and guided his head so that his lips were now on her nipples. Quickly, she unbuckled his belt and slid his pants down; Marco began touching and feeling all over her body, pushing her across the bed. Lourdes started massaging his inner thighs while licking and kissing the side of his neck. She slowly moved her way down to his most-prized possession until she was on her knees, leaving behind a trail of kisses. Seeing his reaction, she smiled as she opened her mouth and closed her lips around his dick, moving her tongue making circles around the head.

Allowing her saliva to drip down, she grabbed his dick with her tongue teasing the head using gentle movements. Marco was feeling good; he flipped her over and slid his dick in from behind. Lourdes was moaning and groaning, trying to maneuver toward the head board but Marco drug her back down in his direction.

When Marco finally hit his groove and stroke pattern, it literally drove Lourdes insane. She was bellowing screams at the force of his dick inside her; she grabbed the bed and ripped a hole in the sheets. After fifteen minutes of spine-busting sex in the doggie style position, Marco went from slow and easy to a no holds barred, all out, full speed thrust from behind. He breathed deeply, filling his lungs with the moist air blowing from the air conditioner as he turned to face Lourdes and they continued to have sex in other positions. Seeing her smile gave him the confirmation that everything was going to be all right.

"Damn girl you're like the energizer bunny, you just won't stop will you?" Marco laughed while he was huffing and puffing, trying to catch his breath.

Marco's cell phone kept ringing. After the fourth call, he looked over to see who was calling…it was Phoenix, and instantly, he felt guilty. "I gotta go."

He sat on the bed, holding the sheet firmly around his waist. He grabbed his boxers that were nearby and put them on.

"Damn it's like that?" Lourdes wore a huge grin on her face. Her hair was a mess and she was trying to slow down her breathing, but she couldn't get herself together because over the course of the day, she and Marco had sex five times. She turned her head, looking at Marco and was met by a devilish grin. Marco took a deep breath while putting on his shirt; he kissed Lourdes on the top of her head and left the room. It was light when he arrived and dark when he left.

When he walked closer to the front door, he heard Lourdes walking into the living room speaking from behind him. He chuckled when he noticed Lourdes was walking with a slight limp from all the sex they had. "When you coming back?" she asked, her hand now on the front door.

Marco was silent for a moment; he turned around and looked at her. "Soon," he replied, giving her a kiss on the cheek and closing the door to leave.

THE NEXT DAY WHEN MARCO woke up he looked at the clock; it was eleven meaning Phoenix would be pulling in at any moment. She called a few hours earlier and said she would be on the road no later than nine. After they hung up, he went back to sleep. Lourdes had drained him of every ounce of energy he had in his body.

When Phoenix walked in the house, Marco was lying on the couch watching Sports Center.

"Can you help me with the bags in the car?" Phoenix asked, kissing Marco on the cheek. "Marco, do you hear me talking to you?" she said after he didn't respond

"I didn't sleep good last night with you gone." He looked up.

"What? You okay?" Phoenix squinted, looking confused because Marco was acting strange, which wasn't like him "That's not what I asked you?"

Marco turned around facing Phoenix, flashing her one of his gorgeous southern smiles that nearly made her heart melt. "Yeah, I'm good...why you ask?"

But when their eyes met, Marco tried to genuinely smile, but he felt so guilty for what he had done the moment it was hard for him to function properly. "I heard everything you said, you said help you with the stuff in the car and that Christian found the perfect wedding gown for you in the first store you went in." All Marco could do was look at Phoenix; he heard his heart beat pounding through his body.

"What you do last night? I called you but you didn't answer." She tilted her head and Marco wondered if she could see, knowing what he had done.

"Nothing I sat right here and watched TV," Marco replied. "Plus my phone died." Marco was feeling guilty, his conscience was telling him that he did something wrong and, it wasn't going to end with last night.

There was no turning back.

PHOENIX
12

$\mathscr{P}$hoenix slammed the bedroom door and dropped down on the bed.

"Fuck him," she mumbled, grabbing her cell phone to dial Reese's phone number.

"Hey girl, what you doing?" Phoenix angrily asked, not meaning to take her frustration out on her friend.

"Nothing just walked through the door from Beachwood Mall."

"Did you find anything good?" Phoenix asked, not paying attention to the conversation she was having with Reese because her mind was focused on being mad at Marco.

"Yeah, Nine West was having a sale and I found a cute pair of heels from Aldo's."

A few minutes later Phoenix heard a knock on the closed door.

"Fee, you act so immature sometimes."

She shot a stern look at the sound of the annoying voice coming through the door as if she was looking directly at Marco.

"Leave me alone," she said.

"Fee, unlock the door and stop being silly," Marco yelled through the door.

"Let me call you back," Phoenix announced to her friend who was holding on the line listening to Marco and Phoenix going back and forth.

"Why do I even bother arguing with you? You don't listen to shit I say anyway."

Phoenix yanked opened the door and looked at Marco from the corner of her eye; she was breathing harder than she needed to because she was very upset.

"Are you fucking serious?" she said. "You ain't talking about shit, so I don't have nothing to listen to."

"Whatever man, with yo' stubborn ass," Marco said with a slight chuckle as he walked down the stairs and out the door.

Their first year living together was a roller coaster and if they didn't truly love each other, they probably wouldn't have lasted. Phoenix's relaxed housekeeping versus Marco's obsessive cleaning habits caused a war. Phoenix was ready to end the relationship several times because Marco constantly complained about her leaving piles of shoes by the front door, clothes on top of the dryer and clothes hangers that she left on the bedroom floor. She felt like Marco needed to loosen up a bit and he felt like she was being lazy.

The next morning Phoenix walked down the stairs into the kitchen to find Marco gone. She felt something had been off, from the moment she had opened her eyes that morning. She thought she was just being paranoid from being exhausted, stressed, and frightened from all this wedding stuff, but her instincts told her differently. She went through her daily routine as usual, but her entire day seemed weird. She was on edge, unsure of what it was that was really bugging her.

When she got home from work, Marco wasn't home. She shook her head; she was thinking too much again. Trying not to let her mind wander, she made her way up to the bedroom determined to get to the bottom of her uneasiness. When she heard the front door open and Marco walk through the door rattling his keys, she made her way back down the stairs to greet her fiancé'."Where have you been?" Phoenix demanded, sounding like a mother scolding her child as soon as Marco walked in the door.

Marco slightly jumped at the question because the sound of Phoenix's voice was very harsh.

"What?" he asked, confused.

"Where were you?"

"At the mall," Marco said without looking directly at Phoenix.

"Umm, is that so?"

"Umm, is that so, what the fuck is that supposed to mean?" he asked. "Fee, where is all of this questioning coming from?"

"I can ask you whatever I want."

"Well fuck it then, if you don't believe me, then what do you want me to do? I told you where I was."

"Fuck you, Marco. Just fuck you," Phoenix said strongly as she walked away.

"Wow it's like that. Phoenix? What's up? Is something wrong?" Marco asked as he followed behind her.

"Do you want to call off the wedding?" she turned and yelled.

Marco didn't answer. Instead, he grabbed Phoenix and hugged her and she reciprocated the hug as she began crying on his shoulder. After feeling her start to calm down, Marco broke the hug and looked into her eyes.

"Fee, I want to marry you, did something happen today? Why are you crying?" he asked, wiping the tears from her cheek.

"Well you need to act like it. We've argued more over these last few months than we have over the course of our entire relationship." She paused and then bluntly asked, "Are you happy with me?"

Marco looked up he was a very confused with Phoenix's line of questions. "Of course I'm very happy with you. I'm madly in love with you." Phoenix stared at him without saying a word as he gently touched her shoulder.

Phoenix's voice began to tremble. "Marco, are you cheating?" She broke into tears again.

Marco was speechless; he couldn't believe what Phoenix just asked him.

"Fee, I promise you everything will be all right, trust me. Right now you're stressed from all this wedding stuff, you need to calm down." Marco kissed her on her head. "It will all be over soon." When she heard silence, she brought herself back to reality after drifting away from the conversation she was having with him. Because he still didn't answer her question, if he was cheating.

Phoenix wasn't sure what was going on, she couldn't imagine living without Marco; they shared something special. In question was if Marco still felt the same way about her. Phoenix wanted to avoid another escalated argument and she wanted to clear her mind.

"I'll be back shortly," she said, grabbing her keys and walking out the house, leaving Marco there wondering what just happened.

MARCO
13

"*I* love you too, baby" Marco whispered on the phone inside the bathroom.

Phoenix stood outside the door and closed her eyes. Marco had just told Phoenix the same thing only an hour prior during their weekly dinner dates.

Phoenix forced herself to look indifferent. "So you love her, huh?" she said, startling Marco as she walked up behind him. He had a look of disgust as he began to open his mouth.

"Fee, I…" he weakly tried to protest.

"I what? Who was that? Phoenix asked coldly, blinking back the tears as she thought to herself, *he will not see my weakness.*

"Wha- What?" Marco asked shocked. *What did she expect me to do act like I didn't t say it?* Marco thought as he stared directly into her face…he was caught.

"I'm done," Phoenix said. Keeping her expression blank, she closed her eyes and let out a deep breath. "I told you there were two things I was not putting up with, cheating and you hitting me." She walked out the room all the while looking Marco directly in his face, her eyes expressionless.

"Phoenix…" Marco was nervous; he chewed on his bottom lip a little and took in a deep breath.

"Who were you talking to?" Phoenix was persistent as she placed her hand on her hip and stared at him.

"Fee, can we talk?"

"Give me your phone and I will call her myself," Phoenix demanded. If looks could kill, Marco would be dead.

"No, I can't do that," Marco responded, shaking his head.

"Then get the fuck out of my face because there ain't shit you can say to me."

"Fee, she's having my baby," he mumbled under his breath.

Phoenix stared at Marco in shock. He felt like his heart stopped for at least three beats and now had jumped to his throat. He didn't mean to hurt his wife; his own words almost brought him to his knees.

"Did you just say she's having your baby? How could that be, we just took vows three weeks ago." Phoenix laughed, trying to mask the hurt.

"Fee, I don't want this marriage anymore," Marco replied with a heavy sigh.

Phoenix's eyes widened then she began to tear up. "Marco, we just got married."

Marco wrapped his arms around her and tried to calm her down, but her body stiffened from his touch and she pushed him away.

"Just let me explain…" He pleaded.

"There is no need right now," Phoenix said with no real concern for anything he had to say. Phoenix looked at Marco as if she wanted to punch him directly in his face. "Right now I wouldn't believe shit that came out your mouth."

"No. Please listen. That is my first child and my baby deserves the opportunity to have both parents in the house because I didn't have that, you know how much that affected me not having my biological father raise me." Marco pleaded, trying to explain himself, but Phoenix's body language showed that she knew he was full of shit.

"Get the fuck out of my face, both parents in the house? What the fuck is that supposed to mean? I didn't have both parents in my household and you had your mother and Bill." Phoenix laughed through her tears after finally calming herself down from all the screaming she had previous done "You hurt me real bad with this one. When I was pregnant you spoke the words abortion so goddamn fast, it was as if you didn't even think about the decision you were making. Remember that shit, how you told me we didn't know each other and you weren't ready. You left me a fucking voicemail telling me about the money you sent through Western Union and the tracking number, remember that shit. Now some bitch says she's pregnant with your baby and you're throwing away us for her. Fuck you." Tears flowed freely down her face.

Marco felt stupid, weak, useless and worthless. Phoenix's voice choked and she could barely swallow as she continued to speak. "I forgave you for just assuming I was having an abortion, I gave us a chance at building a relationship, I trusted you, I took vows with you. You disgust me."

"I didn't...I wasn't...I'm sorry Fee things turned out like this. I never meant for this to happen but I'm going to try and build something with her for the sake of the baby," Marco said in a weak tone not knowing what to say, so he grabbed Phoenix's arm.

How dare he touch me, Phoenix thought to herself. She felt trapped inside all this madness and chaos that people called reality.

"So you're giving up on your marriage for that bitch? Marco, you allow a bitch off the streets to come in and tear down what we've built and now you're leaving your marriage?" Phoenix angrily questioned.

Marco looked over at Phoenix while nodding. "Fee, me and her have a bond now, we're having a baby, she's my baby mama. No matter what happens between me and her in the future, we're going to always have something because we've experienced something major together."

Phoenix sighed as she took in every word that Marco spoke. "Bond, you sound like a damn fool, so us planning a future together wasn't enough for you? We could have been a family years ago but remember you were the one who said you weren't ready to be a daddy so fuck you and yo' baby mama."

"Fee, stop blaming me, I didn't force you to have the abortion. If you truly wanted to have that baby, you would have. We could be parents already had you not had the abortion."

"You, selfish ungrateful son of a bitch! How dare you stand in my face and say some bullshit like that." Phoenix yelled "So you're trying to blame me now for your cheating?"

"I'm sorry I didn't mean it like that. I just need to do what's right for this situation." Marco reached out for Phoenix

"Don't touch me, yes you did. You meant every word you said. If you truly had a problem with me having the abortion we should have had this conversation before today. Hell before we got married" Phoenix yelled as she yanked her arm and Marco immediately backed away. "Leave me alone!" She grabbed her keys and left out the house. Marco watched Phoenix from out the window; he felt drained and empty because everything happened so fast and he had no clue what direction his future was going.

PHOENIX
14

How ironic Alicia Keys' song, "A Woman's Worth," played on the radio as Phoenix cruised down I-271, eyes bloodshot from crying non-stop for the last hour. As she cruised down the highway, Phoenix replayed the conversation she had with Marco over and over again in her mind. She wanted to know who, what, when, where and why of this whole situation. She also thought about the life she'd lived that led her up to this moment. She didn't live a picture perfect life; in fact, to the average person it was fucked up, but in Phoenix's eye she was a survivor, not another problem child from the ghetto. But at this moment she would give anything to be able to snap her fingers and appear curled up in her bed next to her loving husband.

Phoenix pulled into the apartment complex where Reese lived; she desperately needed a friend at that moment. She rang the door bell and Reese rushed to the door probably thinking it was her boyfriend. She unlocked the door and opened it, surprised to see Phoenix standing there.

"Marco cheated." Phoenix cried, looking straight ahead, her expression was blank and distant. She felt numb.

"Oh…Fee, I'm so sorry," Reese said, pulling Phoenix into the apartment and hugging her tightly. Phoenix didn't say anything; she let Reese hold her as she cried quietly.

"He cares only about himself," Phoenix repeated over and over. Phoenix experienced cheating from a previous relationship and she forgave once before, but this time was different. She wasn't going to forgive Marco; he didn't deserve her. Phoenix thought, once a cheater, always a cheater. Reese got on the phone and within the hour both Candy and Shawna were ringing her door bell.

"Oh, look at my poor baby. Do you want to go fuck him up?" Shawna eagerly asked as she wrapped her arms around Phoenix giving her a hug.

"No, what we need to do is go beat that bitch ass, she knew he had a wife. I can't stand trifling ass hoes." Candy chimed in while taking off her jacket. "Do I need to keep this on because we can roll out?" Candy continued while pointing at her jacket.

"I'm not going to jail over this shit." Phoenix looked up at them.

"He fucked her raw dog! No offense, but your husband is dumber than I thought," Shawna announced. "So when is this maybe baby due?"

"So what you gonna do?" Reese asked Phoenix, while giving Shawna the evil eye.

"I don't know. All I know is my marriage is over. I love my husband, I really do love him."

They all laughed in unison at Phoenix's last comment.

"Bitch, your marriage ain't over. That nigga just cheated and left a baby behind," Candy spoke between her laughter

"But he said he was leaving to go make a family with her," Phoenix said, slyly trying to play off her ignorance.

"Don't believe that shit, men talk shit all the time. By the end of the week, he will come to his senses and that bitch will be old news," Shawna said

"How does he even know it's his baby? That bitch could've been fucking everybody in the neighborhood. Do you even know who she is?" Candy added.

Phoenix looked back and forth at her friends. "I don't know nothing about her. The only thing he said was she's having my baby and they were going to be a family."

"Don't let his ass just come back, make him work for it. Make his ass prove that he wants you and only you," Reese said while standing up to walk into the kitchen.

Shawna looked at Phoenix. "Who he think he is, a playa? I would call his bluff and let his black ass go over there and play baby daddy and mama and let him see that the shit ain't all that everybody think it is," Shawna spoke angrily. "What? This kind of shit pisses me off," she replied after noticing Reese looking and laughing at her.

"You crazy, you know that?" Reese said, laughing at Shawna.

"He ain't no playa, just a real good liar," Candy said.

"We were just at your wedding, what three weeks ago? That means she was pregnant before you got married, so he was fucking around. So why in the hell did he even show up to the wedding?" Reese asked, shaking her head in disgust.

Candy added her two cents: "Because he ain't shit and he probably thought he could get away with it."

"This is so ignorant," Shawna yelled, frustrated. "I feel like the shit happened to me. You a better one than me because I would be over there right now going on top of his head, fucking him up."

Phoenix spent the next three hours over Reese's house crying. When she arrived home, she walked into the house, sat her keys on the kitchen counter, and took a quick look around the townhouse. Marco was gone. Something in Phoenix knew he would be gone. The house was empty.

Later...I'll deal with this shit tomorrow, Phoenix thought to herself as she walked upstairs to her bedroom.   As Phoenix undressed to jump into the shower, her attention was caught by a photograph that was staring at her. It was an image of her in her wedding dress and Marco in his tux, both looking happier than ever. Phoenix smiled weakly at the photo and began walking toward the bathroom but before leaving the room she turned and walked toward Marco's closet. She opened the door and let out a tiny gasp when she noticed the majority of his clothes and shoes were gone.

"Damn," she softly said. She immediately called him and wasn't surprised when it went to voicemail.

"Go ahead and leave," she began, "but remember you agreed to this marriage. I didn't force you to get married."

Right now she wanted to turn this entire situation around, but she had no control so she had to settle for crying herself to sleep.

THE NEXT MORNING PHOENIX WOKE up around six and before leaving her bed, she dialed Marco's phone, but the call went straight to voicemail. Next she dialed her manager and called off from work; she had never cried so much as she had the previous night and her body was aching. Phoenix was confused and unaware at that moment who she wanted to call. She dialed a number and waited for the *hello*.

"Hey, you gon' be home?" Phoenix asked

"Yeah, I'm not going anywhere. Why?" Annette replied, still sounding sleepy.

"Because, I'm on my way over."

"All right."

Phoenix hung up the phone and opened her closet and sifted through looking for a decent comfortable outfit; she chose her all black BEBE sweat suit and grabbed her black and white Adidas out the box that was stacked with all her other shoe boxes in the second bedroom.

The drive to her mother's house was a short fifteen minute ride spent in silence and her mind was going a mile a minute. Phoenix wasn't sure what to say to her mother and she was struggling to keep from crying once again. Once she reached her destination, she parked her Honda Accord in her mother's driveway, and she sat in the car staring up at the house she grew up in thinking about how she was going to tell her mother what happened yesterday. She thought about how her life had changed so much in the last twenty-four hours. As Phoenix got out the car and walked in the house, she walked into the smell of bacon and eggs being prepared in the kitchen.

Annette smiled at Phoenix. "What brings you over here so early in the morning?"

"Ma, Marco's having a baby with some woman." Sadness filled Phoenix's eyes.

Annette had a surprise look on her face, but she remained calm, "Damn! Y'all just got married. Is he sure the baby's his?"

"I guess he knows the baby's his because he told me he was leaving me."

"Is there any way you two can work this out?"

Phoenix cried harder. "I don't think so. We really haven't talked much about it. I just found out last night. All he said was he's having a baby, he was sorry for hurting me, and that he was leaving."

Annette listened closely to her daughter's every word. She hadn't been the best mother when her kids were growing up because of her own selfish reasons, but right now she made a personal promise to herself to put Phoenix's wellbeing at the top of her priority list.

"When I came home last night, he was gone and most of his clothes and shoes were gone." Annette held Phoenix in her arms as Phoenix cried on her shoulder. Phoenix cried her heart out and now Annette was crying right along with her.

"You're a strong woman, much stronger than me," Annette said. "It's gonna be all right, you know that right, Fee?" Annette's words were serious; it was rare that anyone saw this side of her.

Phoenix released a huge breath of air, even though she wouldn't admit it to her mother she was embarrassed at the fact that her marriage was possibly coming to an end and if anything she did or didn't do was the reason behind Marco's infidelity.

MARCO
15

Marco hadn't called Phoenix except for the occasional voicemails he would leave asking about his mail and unpaid bills. He couldn't face her; he was too embarrassed. Every time she called his phone, he would send her straight to his voicemail and never returned any of her repeated messages.

Marco finally found the courage to tell his parents what happened, so he flew home to New Orleans to visit them, even though he had just seen them at his wedding less than two months ago. He had to tell them in person about what was going on with his marriage, the baby and him cheating.

"Here we go," Marco whispered as a smile touched his face when he saw his step-father approach the door. "Hey Pops, what's going on?" Marco smiled even harder trying to put on a brave face to conceal his worries.

"Hey son, what are you doing here? Did your mother know you were coming because she hasn't mentioned anything to me?"

Marco considered his parents to be his most trusted friends and even with that being said he still wasn't ready or prepared to answer the questions he knew they would ask.

"No this is a surprise visit," Marco answered, trying hard not to sound sad.

"Where is your wife?" his father asked.

"In Cleveland, she couldn't make this trip." Marco cleared his throat, trying to fight back his tears.

"Baby who's at the door?" his mother called out.

"Marco," his father replied.

Marco lowered his face as he heard his mother's footsteps approaching.

"OOOOH baby, what are you doing here? Why didn't you tell us you were coming?" Mrs. Sutton smiled as she ran up and hugged her eldest son.

The stress, worry, fear and pain that Marco was feeling poured out through his voice. "I have something I need to tell both of you, and I felt I had to do it face to face."

Mrs. Sutton looked at her son with concern and suspicion mixed together. "Come in here and sit down. What is it, baby?" she asked leading Marco into the living room with her husband following close behind.

"I cheated on Phoenix and got another woman pregnant. I just found out about the baby after we came home from our honeymoon." Marco looked at his parents; his mother's face was flushed and his father's eyes were slightly red.

"So when is this baby due and who is this young lady?" she asked. "How is Phoenix handling all of this?"

His father stood in silence, looking at him.

"The baby is due around the end of March or somewhere around that time," Marco replied. "Ma, it's a long story on how I met her. It just shouldn't have happened. I feel so bad because I really hurt Fee. I moved out of the townhouse and now I live with Lourdes, that's her name."

"You know I'm disappointed at you." Mr. Sutton turned around but never looked at Marco.

"I'm sorry, Dad, it was a mistake," Marco replied, quickly looking over at his father.

"Son, how did you allow this to happen?" his father asked. "I thought you two were doing well considering you just got married." Mr. Sutton shook his head in disbelief.

"Hmm Bill." Mrs. Sutton scrunched up her face at her husband's last comment as she turned to face Marco.

"Ma, I'm trying to handle this situation the best way I can. I've never been involved in anything like this before." He looked at his mother; her facial expression turned from a smile to worry. "I'm sorry. I don't know how this happened. I love my wife, I want to be with my wife, but I also want to do what's right for my child." Marco's voice began to shiver

"There is no need to apologize, we love you, son," Mr. Sutton said as he hugged Marco who was now crying on his shoulder.

"So when are we going to meet this young lady that's having our first grandchild?" his mother asked.

"Probably after the baby is born." Marco's mind was everywhere, he felt overwhelmed with all the stress he was dealing with lately. He spent the next two days in New Orleans visiting his family catching up on everyone's life; he played basketball with his little brother and even hung out with his friends AJ and Tyron going to the club. He brought both AJ and Tyron up to date on the drama with Phoenix and Lourdes but he left out a lot of details about the situation because he knew they would have questions that he probably didn't have answers to. Marco needed this time away to get his mind off the soap opera that awaited him in Cleveland.

When Marco came back from New Orleans, he had
Phoenix on his mind but considering his family questioned her
whereabouts, it was impossible not to think about her. He felt
like his mind was truly playing tricks on him and everywhere
he went Phoenix's beautiful smile was there. But he knew it
was time he moved on with his life, he cheated and to him
after a man cheats the relationship was over; he took the time
while in New Orleans to make the decision to move all of his
clothing and shoes out of the house so he could finally move
in with Lourdes and close the chapter of his life that included
Phoenix.

Marco decided to wait until Phoenix left for work to remove
his clothes and shoes from the townhouse out of respect because
he knew it would be too painful for both of them. When he
walked into the house and into their bedroom, he immediately
felt nervous and sad. It felt cold and empty.

"Time to move on, you made this mess now you have to
deal with it," Marco said. He used the majority of his time
thinking about Phoenix and rambling through her personal
things, instead of doing what he came to do. He picked their
wedding picture up off the dresser and smiled at it, even though
Phoenix had colored his face in with a black magic marker
he could still see how happy they were. He also noticed her
wedding ring sitting on the dresser next to the picture and it
broke his heart that even though he messed up Phoenix wasn't
wearing it anymore.

As he grabbed his clothes out of the closet, he chuckled to
himself because certain articles of clothing that Phoenix had
purchased him weren't in there. He looked through the three
garbage bags full of clothes she had piled in the hallway but
that was just sweaters and t-shirts he left in the dresser drawer.

"Damn she got rid of a couple of my favorite jeans and polo's." Marco shook his head at his own disappointments.

Marco knew he was making a life-altering decision, before he left the town house, he left Phoenix a note letting her know he took his clothes, he left the key on the counter, grabbed a piece of fruit and walked out the door having made, a decision he will probably regret as long as he lived.

Marco had officially taken up residence with Lourdes and her kids; a decision he once thought was the right one but was immediately turning into regret. He wasn't getting the proper rest he needed, he should have been able to get a solid eight hours of sleep but he didn't. Instead, he was up all night because Lourdes' kids were up at all times of the night making all sorts of unnecessary noise. Lourdes knew Marco had to get up early for work but she took on the attitude that her kids came before any man so she allowed them do whatever they wanted day and night.

Lourdes cooked a few meals here and there so Marco coming home to home cooked meals was close to non-existence. Lourdes was becoming bitchier as each day passed. For the most part she didn't cook, clean or work; she sat around the apartment all day watching reruns on BET and gossiping on the phone with her friends. Marco was hurting, he had been angry a lot lately; he thought he should be happy but he wasn't but decided to deal with the decision he had made to be with Lourdes for the sake of his child.

AFTER ANOTHER WEEK OF RESTLESS sleep, Marco was tired of the living situation with Lourdes and her kids. When he woke early in the morning on his one day off from work, Lourdes started right in on him, they started arguing about money, how she was raising her kids to the amount of time her youngest son's father spent over their apartment. But it wasn't until Lourdes took the argument to another level and smacked Marco in the face and then told him to pack all his shit and get the fuck out HER house. In Marco's mind that put an end to the feud they were having because he would never put his hands on a woman but Lourdes was pushing him to the edge.

Marco left the house in a furious rage without saying another word. The more he and Lourdes argued, the more he thought about his wife. It had been four months and three days since the last time he saw Phoenix, his one, his everything, his best friend. He missed her scent and her beautiful smile, ever since he abandoned his marriage he thought about his life, his actions and the life decisions he was making. *He* wanted to see Phoenix more than anything at that moment so he drove to her townhouse and showed up at her front door unannounced, in his mind he wanted to talk about their relationship, or lack of.

The sound of the door bell ringing startled Phoenix "Who is it?" she said but Marco ignored her and kept on ringing the bell. Phoenix opened the door to see Marco standing there ringing the door bell, dressed in Sean Jean from head to toe.

"What's up?" Phoenix spoke without much assurance in her voice.

"How you doing, Fee?" Marco paused to flash a smile at her. "Can I come in?" Phoenix gave Marco a look of indifference, he knew she really didn't want him there but he needed her, he needed a friend at that moment. He knew that there was nothing he could say to change the way Phoenix felt, erase the hurt she was experiencing or remove her from the horrible situation he placed her in.

"Sure." Phoenix replied with an attitude as she opened the door further and watched him step past her. As he walked in the house, he gently brushed up against her. "Next time call before you decide to show up at my door unannounced." Marco looked down at the floor as he listened to Phoenix fuss.

"Is everything okay?" Phoenix asked although not really caring about the answer.

"Yeah, everything is good," Marco said, lying through his teeth, "it's just something I felt shouldn't be discussed over the phone." Marco continued as he followed behind Phoenix into the kitchen. She was puzzled after his last comment. Both Marco and Phoenix sat in the kitchen in silence for a moment, neither really not knowing what to say.

Phoenix looked at Marco for a minute, her facial expression rapidly changing. "So you avoid sitting down and talking to me when I asked you to, and now because you're ready to talk you want to have a discussion with me. Give me a fucking break. So, I'm suppose to just sit down and talk to you and everything will be okay? The only thing we can talk about is putting closure to this situation and moving on apart from each other."

"Closure?" Marco responded without looking at Phoenix.

"Yeah…you know like a divorce, annulment…tie up all the loose ends that were kind of just…left undone when you moved out and didn't come back. You ruined my life!"

"Bay-baby," Marco said slowly.

"Don't. You. Call. Me. That," Phoenix screamed, her pent up anger unleashing. "How dare you? You have the nerve to cheat on me, break my heart, end our marriage and now call me baby? How dare you? How can you just act like nothing ever fucking happened? Give me a muthafuckin' break. You hurt me."

"You're talking as if you hate me," Marco replied; his expression showed his anger and frustration with Phoenix.

Phoenix looked directly into his face. "You inconsiderate bastard, yes I did mean it that way, how else would you talk to your worst enemy?" She rolled her eyes at him.

At first Marco didn't respond to her question; he remained silent, trying to regain his composure. "En…enemy! Wow, Fee it's like that now?" His anger was burning her skin.

"Yes enemy. Did you think we were still best friends?" Phoenix laughed.

Marco frowned. "I don't want to hear that shit. I really fucked up, didn't I?"

"No shit, Inspector Gadget," Phoenix smartly replied.

Marco burst out laughing because Phoenix was always getting little sayings wrong and he always had to correct her. "Sherlock, no shit Sherlock."

Phoenix looked at Marco as if she didn't think any of this was funny. "Who is this woman? Do I know her? What's her name?" Sweat started pouring out of the Juicy Couture tank top she was wearing.

"Her name is Lourdes and you don't know her. Believe me when I say, you two do not run in the same circle."

"Then where did you meet her?"

"It doesn't even matter. Phoenix, I'm sorry, I'm sorry I know this probably won't mean much and you probably won't forgive me, but I wanted to at least say I'm sorry. Believe me I never set out to hurt you. Things just got out of control. I…do want you to know why I cheated and what really happened."

"Why Marco, why did you cheat, because you're trifling?"

"Damn why do you always have to add hurtful shit?" He groaned.

Phoenix opened up her mouth to speak, but Marco held up his hand for her to shut her mouth. For once, she did.

"Phoenix. Look, I cheated on you…because…" Marco breathed in deeply and looked Phoenix directly in the eyes. "Because….I allowed another woman to boost my ego. She made me feel wanted." Marco wanted to see Phoenix smile again. And a tiny part of him, wanted to be there for every minute of it but he knew he had hurt Phoenix and he didn't know how to fix the situation.

"Made you feel wan…" Phoenix was cut off from talking, yet again. Marco held up his hand for the second time.

"Not that you weren't doing all the right things. To sum it up she was throwing herself at me, she put the pussy on the table and I took what she was offering. There was no feelings involved, no relationship nothing. "After Marco finished talking he hung his head, as if he was ashamed. Phoenix looked at him, confused.

"Not that I wasn't doing all the right things, but you left your marriage. Give me a break, so you think I'm a fool?" Phoenix spoke, raising her voice at least two pitches higher.

As, if he could read her mind, Marco said. "Look I understand if you don't believe me. But just, please hear me out," Marco desperately said. Phoenix nodded silently unable to speak.

"I love you, and I still do," he continued. Phoenix opened her mouth to retort, but thought better of it. "You are a wonderful person. You're beautiful, you got a great personality; funny and nice, you're extremely intelligent, oh did I mention you're beautiful, you're a special lady." Marco smiled as he finished speaking and Phoenix sat there with tears in her eyes.

"But why would you cheat on me?" Phoenix demanded. Marco looked shocked as if everything he previously said would've explained everything.

"Fee, I'm not perfect, and I allowed temptation to get the best of me. I wasn't thinking with the right head and at the time I didn't think about the consequences."

"Marco, I loved you because you were you and I was me and we connected. We fit perfectly together. I really loved you."

"Loved?" Marco responded, confused.

"And I…still do."

"You still do what?" Marco asked cautiously.

"I said that I love you." She laughed.

"I love you, too, Fee."

Phoenix looked Marco in the eyes the entire time he spoke. Marco wrapped his hands around her waist, bringing his lips to hers and kissing them. He nibbled, sucked and bit all over her body.

"Sorry," he whispered into her ear as he began unbuttoning her top. "Damn girl, you working with a lot." Marco playfully spoke with a grin on his face as Phoenix's breast popped out of her bra.

Phoenix was speechless as Marco propped her on the sturdy kitchen table, her feet swinging a few feet from the floor. Marco felt Phoenix growing wet, her panties were soaked, and her thighs were parted slightly as she waited for his touch.

Phoenix ran her palm over his freshly cut head while he moved his hands down to the zipper of her pants. Unexpectedly Marco threw Phoenix on her back yanking her pants off.

They removed their underwear and Marco positioned himself and pushed inside of her. He kissed her lips as his thrusts became a little quicker. Phoenix closed her eyes, pushing her head back into the table and raising her hips. The whole world seemed to be shaking as Marco pushed inside her again with a loud moan. His hands gripped the edge of the table while he kept his eyes locked on her facial expression.

"Fuck," Marco said with a raised voice, choking on a moan as he proceeded to cum. He stayed on top of Phoenix, breathing heavily onto her skin.

Marco pulled up his pants and slipped on his shoes.

"I'll call." Marco's face cracked into a huge smile as he kissed Phoenix on the cheek before turning to leave. "I'll call you tomorrow, okay?"

All Phoenix did was nod her head as her eyes followed Marco out the door.

PHOENIX
16

*T*wo weeks had passed and Marco hadn't called, so Phoenix finally picked up the phone to call his cell phone.

"It couldn't be," she said. "I know it's not."

She was hearing what she wanted to hear. Marco was being silly and playing games with her. She hung up and called right back.

"The number you have dialed is no longer in service," the automated male voice said.

Phoenix turned on her side, staring out the window; she was embarrassed and felt some type of way that she had allowed Marco to play with her emotions once again by allowing him to her house professing his love, having sex with her and then changing his phone number.

Her phone began to ring on the dresser, knocking her out of her deep thought; she quickly jumped up to get it, her heart beating tremendously fast at the thought of it being Marco.

It was Shawna calling. Phoenix was a little disappointed but relieved that Shawna was calling so that she could get her mind off Marco for once.

"Hey Shawn." Phoenix voice was full of sadness.

"Hey girl, are you feeling okay?"

"I'm fine." Standing, Phoenix let out a huge sigh. It was a brief silence between the lines and then Shawna began to speak.

"Well, me, Reese and Candy are going to Lancer's to eat and I think it will be good for you to get out of the house. Help get your mind off of things."

"Yeah you're right, come pick me up." Phoenix said so quietly that Shawna could barely hear her.

"Okay we will be there within the hour."

Phoenix hung up the phone, looked in her closet, and grabbed her low cut bronze shimmery sweater and a pair of True Religion jeans. It took her the entire hour to get dressed. When she heard the horn blowing, she brushed on her bronze Mac eye shadow and finished her lips with her favorite Oh Baby. She grabbed her keys off the counter and walked out the door.

"Damn girl, you look cute, you got a date or something tonight?" Shawna asked, smiling at Phoenix.

Phoenix grinned from ear to ear. "Nope, but I might meet me a new potential tonight." She teased.

"I ain't mad at you," Reese added as she sped out of Phoenix's apartment complex.

"You doing okay? We haven't really heard from you in a while," Candy asked.

Phoenix put on a fake smile and nodded her head slowly. "Yeah, I'm doing all right." She didn't want her friends to know that she was on the verge of having a major break down. She cried on her drive to work, in her car on her lunch break and on her drive from work. She was taking this entire situation with her and Marco very hard.

"Have you talked to Marco?" Candy asked.

Phoenix rolled her eyes at the thought of hearing Marco's name. "Not in about two weeks. Fuck him, he is truly on my shit list right now."

"This entire situation is fucked up," Reese said. "He had to be fucking with her for a minute." Everyone shook her head in agreement. "What man is just going to leave his wife because some random chick said she was pregnant with his baby? I don't care how many ways you twist it, that is just downright wrong. So when is the Maybe Baby due date again?"

"His mother told me March," Phoenix answered.

"Damn, March is right around the corner, but my question is why is he coming to you like he wants to work on his marriage but at the same time he still lives with her?" Shawna asked.

"Every nigga I fucked with would have been like holler at me when the baby is born and we will go from there. They would have hid that shit like it was the plague." Candy laughed at her own words.

"This shit ain't cute," Reese chimed in even though she had told Phoenix many times how much she liked Marco as a person. Right now she considered his actions to be selfish.

"He's a liar," Phoenix mumbled. "Change in subject, Reese, I've been meaning to ask how is life at Euclid Park Elementary?"

"Just peachy, them damn third graders whine all the damn time. Ms. Jones he touched me, Ms. Jones she cut me. For a bunch of eight and nine year olds they act like two year olds." They all laughed at Reese's funny impression of her students. Phoenix spent many afternoons over the last two years visiting Reese's classroom and she considered her friend to be a hell of a good teacher. Reese had passion and love for teaching, and it showed every day when she entered her classroom.

During dinner with her friends, the only thing Phoenix could think of was the conversation she had with her friends in the car. She wanted revenge, and she wanted it bad. She wanted to hurt Marco like he had hurt her. Even though she knew it was wrong, she didn't care. She would deal with the consequences at a later date.

"Take me to Garden Valley," she demanded.

Reese did a double take. "Garden Valley apartments off Kinsman? For WHAT?"

"That's where my husband lives now and I want to visit him or maybe just go and fuck his truck up a little."

"Oh hell naw, that's the damn projects," Reese said. "There ain't nothing but killas and dealas out there." Reese frowned at Phoenix through the rearview mirror; she was not happy about driving her car to the projects, but she also wasn't against helping her friend.

"Wait a minute, how do you know where he lives because I know he just didn't hand over the address to yo' crazy ass," Candy jokingly asked.

"Bitch, I'm slick, I got the address off a piece of junk mail. The last time he was at my house, he put some papers in the trash and among those papers was that blue value pack with the address posted right on the front. I drove past there a few times just to make sure that was indeed his address and every time I went there his truck was posted up in the parking lot." Phoenix smiled, proud of her detective work.

Shawna turned, facing Phoenix, not wanting to show how scared she was. "Umm, they kill people in the damn day time over there. Do you think they would second guess killing us for sneaking around at night?"

Candy burst into laughter. "I can't believe a nigga with a college degree that works for a large corporation like Nestle ends up living in the projects."

Phoenix answered, poking out her lips, "Me either."

Candy asked, "Who in the hell is this chick? That bitch must do a hell of a lot of tricks in bed to get him to move to the Valley."

As they pulled into the parking lot of the apartment complex where Marco lived, Phoenix immediately spotted Marco's truck parked next to the dumpsters. "See, look at that shit. He's asking for someone to come vandalize his shit, you hear that?" Phoenix placed her hand on her ear being sarcastic.

When Phoenix stepped out the car, her stomach dropped. Currently playing in her mind was "Everything he told me was a lie." They all got out of the car and walked toward Marco's truck.

"Damn, I can't run fast!" Shawna whined as she looked up quickly when they saw lights from a car that was pulling into the parking lot. Shawna was trying to run as fast as she could without tripping in her high heels.

"Run Forest run," Reese teased Shawna as they ducked down behind the dumpsters until the coast was clear.

As they waited behind the dumpster, Phoenix pulled the spare key she found in the kitchen drawer out of her purse and unlocked the doors to Marco's truck. Phoenix jumped in the truck and broke off the turn signal handle and snatched out the light dimmer switch. Candy poured two bottles of motor oil in the gas tank, Shawna broke off both of the windshield wipers, and Reese took a hammer from her trunk to break the glass off the instrument panel.

"This'll teach his ass!" Candy said, busting the lights on the truck with a bat. While Reese and Shawna flattened the tires on the driver's side of the truck, Phoenix took pleasure in listening to the loud deflating sound of both tires on the passenger side hiss as the air seeped out. When it was all said and done, the four friends smiled at their work of art.

FOUR WEEKS HAD PASSED SINCE Phoenix's last communication with Marco and that was via email; he sent her an email message asking how she was doing and to tell her how much he missed her. Not once did he mention why he changed his phone number, and he didn't even offer to give her his new phone number.

Phoenix wasn't bothered by the email because she knew that Marco was playing emotional games, but she was concerned because he never asked nor mentioned the incident that occurred with his truck. Phoenix took it as him just thinking that someone in the neighborhood vandalized his truck and the thought pissed her off because he knew how much he hurt her, but she had no clue how the damage on to his truck affected him.

MARCO

17

Marco felt bad for cheating and hurting Phoenix, his
wife the one woman he truly loved and who he knew truly
loved him, the person her took vows with, the woman he never
meant to hurt but wanted to love forever for a woman that
he barely knew anything about, barely liked and barely could
stand being around. Marco wasn't sure, but he had a feeling
that Phoenix resented him for ruining her life.

"Why did this happen?" Marco asked himself. Tears rolled
down his cheek "This was me and Fee's dream. We were going
to have the perfect family."

He sat in his truck in the parking lot of his apartment
complex, eating his McDonald and silently praying. "God,
please give me strength because if I walk in this house today
and this bitch disrespects me, I swear I'm going to choke her
up, baby or no baby."

When Marco nervously walked in the house, he instantly
got upset. Lourdes had on the same dirty clothes that she'd
worn for the last two days, the kids were running around the
house screaming, and again she didn't cook.

"What happened to the clothes I bought you?" Marco
asked.

132

"Still in the bag, I plan on returning them once I have the baby."

"What! Then why in the fuck did we go out and buy them?" Marco angrily asked.

"That was what you wanted to do. I told you I didn't need new clothes."

"Lourdes, any time when you have to walk around with your pants unzipped because they won't fit over your stomach, they are too small." He paused trying to regain his thought. "This shit is ridiculous," Marco mumbled under his breath. "Yo' trifling ass need to get up and clean up around here," he raised his voice.

"How the fuck am I supposed to do that when I'm nine months pregnant? You clean up if you have a problem with my housecleaning."

"No, what the fuck I'm gon' do is pack my shit and leave." Marco tried to push his way past Lourdes as she stood blocking the front door.

"Your ass ain't going nowhere," Lourdes taunted, the smirk she wore never left her face. "You have a baby to take care of. You can play that shit with your wife, but over here in order to bounce you're going to pay me."

Marco was surprised by Lourdes' reply, but he remained calm. "I'm leaving because I want my life back."

Lourdes laughed. "Baby, take a look around, this is your life. You have a baby on the way, you're first born, only child." Marco hated that Lourdes held the baby over his head; he was in no mood to argue with her or comment on her last statement, so he unbuttoned his shirt, went into the bedroom and lay across the bed.

Lourdes walked in the room

"Are you going to find a job after the baby is born?" Marco calmly asked.

"No, for what?" Lourdes shook her head.

Marco was really irritated with Lourdes' ghetto antics; he wanted to kick his self every day for falling for her. It was like she had some kind of power over him and she was the only one who could release the hold.

"So what are you planning to do then?" he questioned but Lourdes turned and walked away without so much of a hint of her future plan.

MARCO HEARD A LOUD SCREAM in the middle of the night. Lourdes was crying in pain as she went into labor. The doctors had told them she could have the baby soon, so Marco assumed the baby would probably come any day now, so he barely slept at night.

"Baby, it's time to go?" Lourdes whined as she stood holding her stomach, her hand just underneath her lower stomach.

Marco grabbed his jogging pants, called the neighbor to watch the kids and drove as fast as he could to University Hospital. Marco didn't know what to expect; he thought as soon as she went into labor, the baby would come right out. He was wrong; Lourdes was in labor for six hours. They did agree on one thing, a natural birth with no epidural. Marco wanted the best for his future child.

"Wow I'm about to be a daddy." Marco smiled to himself as he broke down in silent tears.

He stood over Lourdes bed, smiling. "Give me your hand," Lourdes said, smiling as Marco placed his hand on her stomach, suddenly he felt multiple kicks which made him think back to the day Lourdes told him she was pregnant…that was the happiest day of his life.

"Phoenix, try and push," Marco pleaded. Lourdes took a deep breath and pushed as hard as she could. Marco's face froze after he realized he called Lourdes by the wrong name.

"I need you to push one more time, the baby's crowning," the doctor announced.

"I can't." Lourdes sighed, sweat rolled down her face.

"Come on, baby, do it for us," Marco begged as Lourdes closed her eyes and pushed as hard and quickly as she could. When Marco heard the sound of the baby crying, tears formed in his eyes. He was extremely happy.

"It's a girl," the nurse announced.

The nurse handed Marco the baby after they wiped her down.

"My first baby girl, your daddy is going to spoil you." Marco smiled as tears rolled down his face. He looked over at Lourdes. They kissed and then he tried to hand her the baby.

"You can hold her," Lourdes said, smiling slightly. Marco felt like she was acting very distant toward the baby. He notices she was avoiding holding the baby and even having eye contact with the baby. When Lourdes and Marco brought the baby home, Marco loved being a new father. He studied, stared and smiled at his daughter every day.

"Are you two going to sit and stare at each?" Lourdes laughed.

Marco leaned forward, looking down at the baby as she lay in the crib. She looked up and was staring back at him. "Yup, until I get tired," Marco replied, smiling.

"I'm going to The Trilogy on Saturday with my sister."

Marco shook his head; he looked kind of sad. "Didn't you just go there the other day?"

"No, I went to the Millennium, so now you trying to control me?" Lourdes asked. "You try being pregnant for nine months and can't go nowhere, then we can talk. Until then I'm going out on Saturday with my sister."

"Why do you always twist my words around? Honestly I don't really care if you go out, but you have a new born at home," Marco said harshly

"Ohh really, then why are you always getting mad when I go out and then you start questioning me?"

Marco looked at her. "I'm not questioning you nor am I mad. Don't you want to stay home and bond with your daughter?"

"We have many years to bond. She will be all right."

Marco took a deep breath, trying to lower his voice so he wouldn't startle the baby. "I don't have time to argue with you right now. I have to feed my daughter."

Lourdes rolled her eyes. "Okay well I'm out of here, me and the kids will be at my sisters, daddy daycare." Lourdes laughed as she and her three other children left the apartment leaving Marco to care for his daughter by himself.

He looked somewhat disappointed for a few seconds. He was tired of Lourdes' ignorant actions; she just gave birth two weeks ago, and she was already running the streets, leaving him to feed, bathe and put the baby to sleep every night.

PHOENIX
18

*B*y the time Friday rolled around, Phoenix was mentally and emotionally exhausted and was looking forward to Happy Hour with her friends. Reese had texted earlier to confirm they were still meeting up for drinks.

"There they are," Phoenix spoke to Reese over the extremely loud music as they entered the bar. They walked over to the table where Candy and Shawna were already seated.

"Happy Hour is jumping tonight," Phoenix commented. "Have y'all order yet?" She watched the waitress walk over to their table.

"How are you tonight, ladies?" The waitress smiled while she took their drink orders.

"How's law school, Ms. Candy?" Phoenix asked.

"I can't wait to finish. It's been hard, but the payoff is coming real soon," Candy responded, grinning from ear to ear.

"Can we go out tonight?" Shawna interrupted, dancing in her seat to "How We Do" by The Game.

Phoenix looked at Shawna with disgust because she was being rude.

"But anyway," Phoenix continued talking turning her attention back to Candy. "Candy I'm going to need a divorce lawyer, so I need you to hook me up with one from the law firm where you're doing your internship."

"So you're really going to divorce him?" Reese asked with genuine interest.

"Good, leave that motherfucker alone!" Shawna blurted out; she was very frustrated with this entire situation "It's not even worth it, but seriously he needs to get himself together. He needs someone sane to talk to because right now he is struggling."

"I am leaving him alone," Phoenix said, frowning at Shawna for a brief moment. "He left me, so what am I supposed to do, sit around and wait for him to come back? Not gonna happen. I'm moving on."

"I will talk with one of the attorneys at work on Monday," Candy replied, smiling.

"Thanks, I appreciate it." Phoenix focused on Shawna who she felt was in need of attention tonight. "I'm going to have to pass on the club tonight. I'm tired, and I had a long week."

"Okay." Shawna pouted.

They sat at the table drinking and laughing until tears rolled down their faces. Candy was making them laugh reminiscing about stories from their childhood and all the sneaky things they used to do.

"We all should be in jail, with the dumb shit we used to do," Candy said, smirking.

Phoenix decided to call it an early night around midnight.

"I'm leaving" She yawned as she stood grabbing her purse and keys.

"Bye babes, be careful," Reese said, smiling, while Candy waved goodbye.

"Layter," Shawna said, laughing.

When Phoenix got home, she couldn't sleep, so she logged onto her computer to check her email. She opened her inbox and raised her eyebrows when she saw Marco had sent her a message.

"This is the type of shit that pisses me off. Now we're down to communicating through email." Phoenix shook her head. "I'm over this shit." Suddenly her face fell when she looked at the email again and read the subject line and who was all included in receiving the email.

"What the fuck!" Phoenix screamed out loud. She was pissed. Her chest was tightening up, she thought she'd never breathe again and she was fairly sure she had steam coming out of her ears. She hadn't been this mad in a long time. She tried to calm herself down by taking deep breaths before she opened the message that she was now facing. The words in the subject line were already enough for her.

"Caaaandy!" Phoenix's voice was shaking through the phone; she was unsure if she wanted to scream or cry. Phoenix was furious. She felt like Marco had played her and she hated that he made her feel like this.

"What's the matter?" Candy asked.

Phoenix was stuttering "That son of a bitch had the nerve to send me a birth announcement to my email!" Phoenix yelled as she wiped away her tears.

"Phoenix, calm down!" Candy demanded.

Phoenix sobbed a little more and continued speaking, "Let me read the email to you. The subject line says Baby News! And the message says Congratulations on my new baby girl Marika Donisha Sutton, born March 21. She was seven pounds three ounces and she's beautiful. Then there is a picture, it looks like it was taken at the hospital."

"Seriously!" Candy asked, shocked. Meanwhile Phoenix was trying to regain her thoughts from what she was now experiencing.

"But what makes it so bad, Candy, is he had the nerve to send out a massive email to his friends and family, so I know they all see that he sent this shit to me."

"What did you expect? He's been doing ignorant shit this entire what seven or eight months," Candy responded. "I have been holding my tongue for a while now, but this situation is getting out of hand. I know you're hurt, but now you have to start taking responsibilities for your actions for the hot and cold way you present yourself and your feelings toward Marco."

"I have taken responsibility," Phoenix responded defensively

"No you don't, Fee, listen to you now. You become extremely defensive when I ask you something about Marco or if I say that something you told me don't sound right. You just mentioned no more than a few hours ago that you were divorcing him, so close that chapter and move on with your life because believe me he's moving on with his life."

"You're right I did say that," Phoenix mumbled.

"Now it's obvious that he's the one who's been lying about what's really going on with this situation concerning that chick and that baby. I'm sure he still loves you and I know you love him, but don't lose yourself in this man or this marriage. Value your worth and demand to be valued by this man. Don't love a man more than you love yourself. Don't define your worth by whether or not you have a man by your side."

Phoenix's mouth fell open. She looked at her cell phone in shock, not knowing whether to be offended or what. "Are you serious?" Phoenix was now angry. "Just forget about it, it doesn't matter. I'll talk to you later." She hung up the phone, trying not to lose her temper over Candy's last statement.

After hanging up with Candy, Phoenix sat at her computer and stared at the email; she needed some time to digest this email and figure out what she was going to say before she responded.

Marco,

I know you are aware I know your baby is born. Of course you do because you sent me this email. CONGRATS ON THE BABY AND ALL THAT. HOW DARE YOU embarrass me in front of all your family and friends by adding me to a birth announcement that included a picture that I was not ready to see? YOU ARE A COWARD.

Fee

Phoenix clicked the send button and shut down her email. She was nervous because Marco had changed so much lately that she never knew what bag he would be coming out of. It took her almost a week to respond because she needed time to sort out her feelings about the entire situation. She was very lonely and sad; she called up Shawna because Shawna would always listen to her and wouldn't point fingers like Candy usually did. Phoenix felt like she had no direction in her life and talking to Candy made it a bit difficult for her to be honest about her true feelings about wanting to work on her marriage.

"Girl, Marco is truly taking me there. I sent him a response to his little birth announcement. I still can't believe that shit."

"You can't believe what?" Shawna asked.

"That he had the nerve to add me to his mass email. That shit was so disrespectful."

"That's because he doesn't respect you. First of all, it's very disrespectful for him to throw his love child in your face. So I guess he said fuck you and your feelings, huh?"

Phoenix sat on the phone in silence; she had just heard the same speech from Candy a few days ago. Even though she knew what they were saying was true, at the end of the day, it was her decision to stay with Marco or leave.

Shawna took a deep breath. "This is becoming too confusing, one day Marco's sorry and wants to work on his marriage and the next day he's back at home with that chick playing daddy. If he was really apologetic, he'd be respectful of your feelings and it doesn't seem like he is or he wouldn't have sent you an email announcing the birth of this Maybe Baby."

"I totally agree," Phoenix said in her I'm really not listening to you tone of voice.

"Fee, you know I will never turn my back on you or refuse to listen without judgment, but you keep saying you don't know what you want to do, but I think you need to let him go. You deserve so much more."

Phoenix was confused because just five seconds ago Shawna said she wouldn't judge her now she was telling her to leave Marco.

Tears started to form in Phoenix's eyes; she was embarrassed by this entire situation. "Hey do you have to work today?" Phoenix changed the subject

"Nope, thank goodness. I have today and tomorrow off." Shawna smiled through the phone.

"Okay, I want to go to the mall later because I need some new work clothes."

"I know The Limited and Macy's are having sales."

Phoenix and Shawna had a great day shopping and just having fun together. Phoenix was always thinking of things to do to occupy her time so she was not focused on the annoying image of Marco flashing through her head all the time.

After a long day of shopping and hanging out with Shawna, Phoenix anxiously sat down at her computer. The first thing she did was open up her email; she had been waiting on Marco to respond. Her inbox was filled with everything from order confirmations, auto bill pay confirmations, junk mail and a hand full of personal emails thrown in from various people including an email from Marco. Marco's email was dated three days ago, but it still took him two weeks to respond. Phoenix read the email carefully, analyzing each and every word which wasn't many because his email was short.

Phoenix,
Yes I fucked up and I've admitted this several times to you. I wish things had happened differently, but they didn't, so I have to go on with life. Thanks for the congrats, but I do apologize. I did not mean to send that email to you, it was a mistake. Please forgive me.
Marco

Marco's email pissed Phoenix off because in her mind she felt like he didn't say anything. She was his wife and he owed her more than a two line email repeating the same shit he always said when he responded and to her his apologies meant nothing to her.

Marco,
So it takes you two weeks to respond back? You're full of shit and my whole outlook on you has changed. I'm no longer in love with you or care what happens to you. All I want is a divorce.
Phoenix

Marco immediately responded back to Phoenix. She wondered if he was waiting by his computer like she was waiting on her response.

Phoenix,
Divorce! Are you serious Phoenix? I think we need to talk, but I've been very busy with the baby. This is all new to me and I'm trying to adjust to everything. Well I'm still in love with you and I hope that what we had was real because I never stopped loving you. Phoenix, I miss having you in my life and I wish I could have you back in my life because you mean so much to me. Maybe we can still sit down one day and talk. I would like the chance to repair my relationship with you. Please tell me there is some hope? Can you please forgive me? I love you, Fee.
Marco

Phoenix bit on her bottom lip; she told herself she wasn't going to cry as she read Marco's email over and over. Phoenix felt like Marco had stabbed her with a knife directly into her heart. How dare he put in an email that he wanted to repair their relationship, when every time she reached out to him to talk about their relationship, he would shut her out, "they say misery loves company and I'd be damn if he's going to continue to hurt me." Phoenix angrily spoke out loud "He gets on my damn nerve, this entire situation is getting on my nerves" Phoenix yelled. "He needs help if he just assumes that I would continue to be married to him. Fuck you that bitch and y'all baby."

Marco,
You walk around like you're the victim and that you have no responsibility in all of this. Do you know how many times you

have said we were going to sit down and talk? Well I do—more than I can count. Repair our relationship? How can we repair our relationship if you're laid up with another bitch every night? The only hope you have for us is having a smooth divorce. Marco, I'm tired of the games. Stop the madness.

Phoenix

Marco replied to Phoenix's email with an invitation to dinner. Phoenix smiled a little after reading the email; she contemplated his invitation before finally agreeing to have dinner with him that Saturday at seven at Ruth Chris on Chagrin Road. Phoenix was nervous the two whole days it took for Saturday to arrive. Candy told her she shouldn't go on the date because Marco didn't deserve to have her friendship.

She was still pissed with Marco from the incident a few days ago in the parking lot at Target on Mayfield Avenue. As Candy was walking into Target, she saw Marco and a female wheeling around a cart filled with household items walking toward the check out line. Candy rushed back outside through the double doors and walked over to Marco's truck. She picked a rock up off the ground and bust Marco's side window. As she was walking away, she bumped right into the two as they approached Marco's truck…she was busted.

"Bitch, what's yo' problem? Why you bust my man's window?" the female standing next to Marco shouted.

Candy slightly smiled as she continued to walk away from Marco's truck.

"Karma" she mumbled because she knew the female with Marco was no other than Lourdes.

"Bitch, what you say? I will fuck you up," Lourdes said.

"You ugly ghetto project bitch! Out here in public looking like you just rolled out of bed with a damn scarf on your head." Candy turned around, waving her hands in the air.

Lourdes was stunned as she turned her head looking at Candy then at Marco. "My man takes good care of me. Why, are you jealous? It must be because I took him away from your little friend and the fact that I'm the one he fucks every night. And he likes it, too." Lourdes grinned evilly.

"Get on my level, dusty bitch, and then come talk to me." Candy whipped her head around in the direction where Lourdes was standing, but kept her eye on Marco daring him to respond; he didn't move a muscle. "Bitch, what goes around comes around."

"What!" Lourdes asked, truly not understanding what Candy meant.

Candy replied, pointing into Lourdes' face, "You heard me, why are you fucking with a married man?" Lourdes ignored the question and just stared at her. "You keep getting all hyped at the mouth and you will get fucked up."

"Get your finger out of my face," Lourdes shouted, grabbing Candy's finger and bending it as far back as she could.

"Let my finger go," Candy screamed before she quickly picked Lourdes up and slammed her on the ground and watched as Lourdes head hit the ground hard.

Marco stood in shocked, shaking his head at the cat fight going on in front of him.

"Someone call 911," Lourdes cried out as she laid on the ground while Candy sat on top of her scratching her face, pulling her hair and tearing at her shirt.

An older man walking past, noticed Marco just standing there looking at Candy and Lourdes fight, so he put down his bags and pulled Candy off Lourdes.

"Lord," Marco mumbled quietly, taking a few steps forward to help Lourdes get up off the ground. Marco remained quiet; he didn't look concerned anymore. He was now angry. "Candy, why you bust my window?" Marco asked, trying to remain calm.

"Bitch, you better not let me see you in the streets," Lourdes threatened, spitting in the direction where Candy was standing.

"Fuck you, sorry ass bitch, I'm here now," Candy yelled. "And your trifling ass *can't prove anything!*" She stuck her tongue out at Marco.

The police arrived, and Marco explained to the officer what happened and then the officer began to question Candy.

"Ma'am, did you bust his window?"

"Nope I didn't do anything," Candy replied.

"Then why do you have several pieces of glass in your hair?" Candy flinched up as the officer pulled glass from her hair... she was caught. "I need to arrest you."

"Arrest me for what?" Candy asked angrily "Get off me, I didn't do anything." The officer proceeded to arrest her for destruction of property. One of the partners at the law firm Candy interns for immediately contacted the district attorney's office and had the charges dropped. Phoenix picked Candy up from the police station and Candy was fuming with anger and she let Phoenix know exactly how she felt. "Have you ever stopped to think how me, Reese and Shawna...your friends thought about this situation?"

Phoenix was confused and nervous; she didn't know what direction Candy was going with this conversation "Yes, I have."

"I don't think so. Even though I have no real justification for my anger, it's there. Do you know I could have fucked up my career over this bullshit? Even though I took action out on his truck, it was all because of the way he's treating you."

Phoenix was speechless; she was torn. She wanted her friendship with Candy, but she also wanted her marriage with Marco. "Candy, I'm so sorry for putting you through this. You're a really great friend. You always have been."

"That bitch had the nerve to brag about not working and Marco taking care of her. I should have fucked her up on the scene just for running her mouth. See, that would have been worth the trip to jail." Candy laughed, giving Phoenix the sign that she was no longer upset. Phoenix was in shock she was definitely in need of a bottle of Zinfandel to relax her nerves.

SATURDAY ARRIVED AND MARCO HADN'T called, but he did send an email message the day before from his work confirming their date. After a long shower, Phoenix looked in her closet to find something cute but classy to wear. She picked up her cell phone; she had two missed calls one from her sister Tasha and the other from a private number, so she assumed the private caller was Marco, but he didn't leave a message.

She looked in the mirror at herself before leaving the house. "I'm too good for Marco anyway."

It was exactly seven when Phoenix pulled up at Ruth Chris. She got out of the car, smoothed out her pants and shirt, and locked up her car. She looked down at herself; she was wearing a pair of black pants, a pink tank top under a short sleeved black jacket, and a pair of pink heels.

Phoenix looked at her watch; fifteen minutes had passed since she arrived at the restaurant.

Where is he? she thought. She really thought he'd changed considering he asked her out to dinner.

Phoenix smiled politely at the waiter. "Can I start you off with a drink?" he asked.

"I'll have water, no lemon" she replied, quickly looking away with an annoyed expression.

Thirty minutes! Phoenix was pissed; she couldn't believe that Marco was not there, but then again it didn't surprise her. "It's because he doesn't really love you" the voice in her head told her. At one point Phoenix thought Marco was *The One.*

Phoenix sat alone in the restaurant for another five minutes then she grabbed her purse and left. She was trying very hard not to cry. When she got into her car, she pulled out her Boyz II Men *Evolution* CD; she clicked on Track 2 and began singing as loud as she could.

"In this world today, love is scarce…"

As she started into the chorus of the song, her cell phone rang. It was Reese. Phoenix was sure she was calling to be nosey, and Phoenix wasn't in the mood to listen to her bad mouth Marco.

Phoenix knew it was time she moved on with her life; she was only twenty-four and still had a full life a head of her. Even though she loved Marco with all her heart, she was not going to allow him to ruin her life; she refused to be a scorn woman who hated men and with Marco's actions she could see herself headed down that road

MARCO
19

$\mathcal{M}$arco listened as Lourdes rummaged through the kitchen, banging pots and pans together sounding as if she was trying to make as much noise as she could.

"Really, so you're just going to be ignorant and make all that noise knowing I'm trying to put the baby to sleep?" Marco asked as he walked into the kitchen to see what was going on.

"You said I don't do shit around here." Lourdes rolled her eyes and continued throwing several pots into the cabinet as her voice echoed into the living room.

"You don't do shit," Marco mumbled as he walked back into the living room and sat down on the couch rocking the baby to sleep.

Lourdes moved quietly but quickly to where Marco was sitting on the couch and stuck a knife in his face just short of sticking him in the corner of his eye. "Who the fuck you think you talking to?" Marco pushed the knife out of his face."

Marco felt his temper heat up as he snapped. "Are you crazy, don't you ever put a knife to my face. I don't know what the fuck those other nigga's allowed you to do, but you won't do that shit anymore especially in front of my daughter."

"Oh so now I'm crazy. Bitch, you better not go to sleep because you will see crazy," Lourdes screamed at the top of her lungs with a strong Spanish accent.

Marco shook his head. "Lourdes, don't you ever threaten me," he shouted.

"Fuck you! You're a sorry excuse for a man and an even sorrier excuse for a boyfriend and father."

Marco stepped back in shock, his eyes widened because her words put a dent in his pride. "Thanks for letting me know that." His voice was emotionless. He swallowed hard as he stared at the floor, struggling to keep tears from forming.

"Why the fuck is your Chase credit card late?" Lourdes asked, changing the subject as if she was finding any way to continue the argument.

"What?" Marco asked.

"The bill came in the mail the other day, so I opened it and it said you were past due."

"Why are you opening up my mail?"

"Because whatever the fuck comes to this address, the address where only my name is on the lease, I can do what the fuck I please."

"Well since your nosey ass must know I can't pay the bill because you always got your hand stuck out for something. *Your* kids always need something and my daughter needs things. So guess what, I don't have any extra money."

"It sounds like you need to go out and get another job."

"No, it sounds like you need to get off your lazy ass and get a job," Marco said, frustrated. He felt like his brain was about to shut down and take a break from all this madness that he lived with every day.

"Oh and tell your mother to stop calling me all day, every day asking about the baby. The answer is the same…she's sleep. What the hell else do she expect a baby to be doing?"

"That was very ignorant of you to say." Marco stood up from the couch.

"Whatever!" Lourdes shrugged her shoulders "Yo' mama ignorant for calling every day."

"I never knew you were so heartless." Marco stared at Lourdes in disbelief

"I'm not heartless! I'm just telling the truth," Lourdes angrily said as she flicked on the television with the remote. "Where are you going?" Lourdes asked as she watched Marco put the baby down in her crib, change his shirt, grab the keys to his truck, and walk toward the front door.

"If you must know, I'm going to Al & Dave's Place off Libby Road." Marco turned and left before he could see Lourdes' reaction.

MARCO SPENT TWO HOURS INSIDE the bar; he felt defeated and was determined to leave every fucked up thought he had about Lourdes right there inside of Al & Dave's, right next to the five shots of Hennessy he drank. His mind was focused on Phoenix; he needed to talk to her. It had been four days since he stood her up by not showing up at the restaurant and he still hadn't called to apologize or say anything. Marco truly couldn't face Phoenix and he didn't want to tell her the reason for him not showing up was because Lourdes up and left the house, leaving him to babysit all the kids from six in the evening until one in the morning.

As he left the bar after having too many drinks, he wanted to use this opportunity to confess to Phoenix that all this time she was right when she told him he was making bad decisions. Every since the day he cheated with Lourdes, he'd been making very bad decisions and he regretted each and every one of them.

Marco sat outside Al and Dave's bar in the Southgate shopping center parking on top of being drunk he felt lonely and needed someone to talk to desperately. Talking to Lourdes wasn't an option because if she wasn't asking for money, all they did was argue about any and everything and calling his friends wasn't an option either because his pride wouldn't allow him to have the type of conversation with them that he needed to have at that moment. The one person he truly felt comfortable talking to was Phoenix but he was too scared and embarrassed to call her because he had ripped her heart out of her chest with all the hurt he caused her.

Marco sat inside his truck that was still parked inside the Southgate shopping center as he dialed Phoenix's phone and listened to the ringing sound on the other end of the phone. When he heard Phoenix's voice suddenly he wanted to hang up the phone but he took the risk and stayed on the phone.

"Hello?" Phoenix answered after the third ring.

"I'm sorry, did I wake you up?" Marco asked tipsy.

"Marco, what's wrong with you? It's after midnight." Phoenix asked in a flat tine

"Do you mind me coming over there? I really need to talk to you and I can't do it over the phone, and I don't want to wait till tomorrow."

There was a long pause. "Naw, it's too late," she replied.

"Well I guess I will tell you now. Please it won't take long." Marco begged, sounding a little Ralph Tresvantish; he was acting real sensitive at that moment.

"Go ahead." Phoenix spoke as if she wasn't feeling any pity for Marco.

"I love you; you know that, don't you?" Marco professed through the phone; he was allowing the liquid courage he drank earlier to build his confident. He wasn't sure what to expect from this phone call, but he took a chance anyway.

"No, Marco, I don't. I don't know anything anymore. I only can go by what you tell me."

"Well I do, I love you with all my heart. I'm feeling so much pain knowing that I've hurt you and caused you pain and even though I don't deserve you, I want you by my side. I'm sorry, Phoenix, can you forgive me?"

"You should know the answer, Marco," Phoenix said. She had already forgiven him; she had to in order to move on with her life. "Where did you meet her again?" Phoenix asked, "So why do you keep calling me professing your love when you live there?"

Marco hesitated. "Craigslist."

"What the fuck did you just say, Craigslist? Do you know the type of people that are on there? Bitches sell all kinds of sexual services on there; anybody who looks for love on Craigslist is desperate." Phoenix sat straight up in her bed, now wide awake.

"I was just on there looking at the pictures, it was nothing. I came across her picture and we emailed back and forth, flirting for a while. She was coming on strong in her emails. I took the bait and one day we just met up at her house."

Phoenix's eyes widened in surprise; her tone was as if her anger was on level ten. "What the FUCK! You had unprotected sex with this random bitch you met on Craigslist. You, nasty, trifling bastard, you could have brought home any and all kinds of diseases including AIDS.

"So the bottom line is you left me for a bitch you met on Craigslist," Phoenix shook her head quickly, trying to get rid of all the thoughts that were passing through her head.

"Fee, I'm sorry." Marco's voiced slurred as he spoke. "She came on strong, I was a challenge to her, a conquest, and it was a little game to her."

Phoenix remained silent; she lay in her bed, staring into space, wondering what the hell she got herself into. "So once again, you're Mr. Innocent. What did I do to deserve this? Why did you ask me to marry you if you were looking for something else? Never in a million years did I think I would hear you say some shit like this. Is this the first time you did this? Are you a pervert?"

Getting over the embarrassment, Marco took a deep breath, his voice sounded almost like he was pleading. "I married you because I love you and yes this is the first time I met someone on there. No I'm not a pervert. It just happened. The situation got out of control."

"You sound ridiculous, you allowed the situation to get out of control; it just didn't happen because you continued to communicate with her. And what's so great about her story that made this situation got so out of control?"

"What? I don't know, Phoenix, her story is all over the place." He tried to avoid the question. "It's nothing to tell."

"Let, me be the judge of that, I still wanna hear it."

"Lourdes, she's thirty-three, and she has four kids including my daughter."

"Wow, four kids! How old are her kids? Where the fuck she work that she can take care of four damn kids by herself?" Phoenix rolled her eyes.

Marco hesitated. "I don't know how she gets money, but she's in between jobs right now and the kids are five, four and three years old and now our baby."

"Do they have the same daddy?" Phoenix asked, unimpressed.

"The first two have the same daddy; and the youngest one has his own daddy and he a young dude, I think he like twenty or twenty-one. But it doesn't matter because none of their daddies is around."

"That bitch is on welfare, I bet she is, especially if she's not working with all those damn kids and why the fuck would she go and have a baby with a damn twenty year old and she damn near forty and now you. Wow, sounds like you have a real winner there." Phoenix was pissed. How could he do this to her? This woman had no money, no job, she lived in the projects and he met her on Craigslist. "Alright I heard enough I'm done with this conversation." Phoenix said as the anger began to rising inside of her body.

"Fee"

"Huh"

"I'm not hanging up this phone until you tell me you forgive me. I miss you I need my friend back, at this point I will take any piece of friendship that you will allow me to have with you." Suddenly all Marco heard was the phone hanging up abruptly.

Marco felt defeated as he sat in his car with his head laid back. His emotions flip flopped all over the place, one moment he wanted to rekindle the love he had for Phoenix and work on his marriage and the next moment he felt like it was his duty to give his child an opportunity to see his or her parents together, he never felt so alone and confused in his entire life.

MARCO
20

MARCO SHOWED UP AT PHOENIX'S door, once again unannounced, and when she opened her door, the anger showed up all over her face. He could tell she was still furious from the information she received from the phone conversation they had a week ago.

"I'm sorry, Fee." After a string of apologies, Phoenix finally allowed Marco inside her townhouse.

"Excuse me for being a little pissed off, but you don't have the right anymore to just show up unannounced! I don't know where you live, I don't have your phone number, so don't call my phone." Phoenix shook her head and rolled her eyes.

"Damn Fee, give me a break, my number is 319-2135." Marco tried to brush it off and move on to the next topic of conversation, but in his mind Phoenix wouldn't let it go.

Phoenix spoke in an angry tone, "What do you want?"

Marco answered in a rather apprehensive tone, "I was thinking about you. I just wanted to see how you were doing."

"So you aren't ignoring me anymore, huh?" Phoenix asked, being sarcastic.

Marco paced around the living room in deep thought. There was so much stress around him these days that he could hardly function. "Fee, I wish this never happened. I'm in a real bad situation. I can't take living there anymore. She makes me so mad with her smart ass mouth."

"That's what you chose, remember?" Phoenix smirked.

Marco shot her a strong look "Let me tell you what happened yesterday. We were arguing as usual over the baby because she is never at home, she is always in the streets and she leaves me at home with the baby. I don't mind because she's my daughter, but still." Phoenix looked at him like she was not interested in hearing his story. "She is always running her mouth so she jumped in my face screaming about the same shit. I can't control her. She started hitting me in the chest, so I shoved her ass up against the wall and then started choking her. Fee, if it wasn't for the baby crying, I don't know what I might have done."

"What same shit?" Phoenix asked, refraining from rolling her eyes because she tuned Marco out the first time he told her the reason for the argument.

"The same shit we always argue about, her not working, the kids, her smart ass mouth, her going out all the time and leaving me with the kids. Where do you want me to stop?" Phoenix looked as if she was going to say something but instead she shook her head as she listened to Marco speak. "After the fight yesterday, I went and stayed at a hotel."

Phoenix stared at her husband, her mouth dropped. "Wow, sounds like you got yourself caught up in a real life *Thin Line between Love and Hate*."

"Yeah, I don't know I can't really explain but it's a bad situation. I had to leave the house before I killed her literally."

Marco stepped closer to where Phoenix was standing. "This shit is fucked up. I'm so miserable. This whole thing was a huge mistake. She is so fuckin' hood, Fee. She is not the person for me. I punched a hole in the wall two weeks ago and in that same fight she threw a plate at me that hit the wall and broke."

"Sounds like you have a project chick, straight hood. Why didn't you use a condom again?" Phoenix asked, looking like she wasn't convinced with Marco's words as she watched his every move. "Why don't you leave me alone, and let me move on with my life?" Phoenix looked at him; her face showed her hurt turning into hatred in a matter of seconds.

"Look shit happens and I hardly have time to think straight anymore," Marco boldly said. "And now her sister is calling my cell phone threatening me, talking about her boyfriend is this big time drug dealer and he gon' do this and that to me."

"Marco I don't care about all that bullshit, they need to beat yo' ass for being so damn dumb. So are you two officially a couple now?" Phoenix asked out of nowhere.

"I don't know, yeah I guess you could say were together but only by default," Marco said defensively.

"Are you in love with her?"

"What makes you say that?" Marco asked. "Yeah I have feelings for her."

"Like you had feelings for me? But my question is do you love her, because that would only explain why you put up with all that bullshit." Phoenix shouted in his face as she walked away.

"What do you mean?" Macro asked, following her into the kitchen. "You're my wife, it's different. That shit over there is crazy."

"Marco please stop acting like you don't understand my question."

"Fee, the question you ask I don't know the answers to."

Phoenix looked around the room with an angry stare. "You don't know if you love this woman who you left me for! You answer needs to be YES because if not than you are just as fucked up as this situation. From what you told me there ain't shit positive about this woman. You don't know shit about this woman like you think you do, you a fuckin' fool," she yelled snapping Marco out of his thoughts.

"Yeah, Fee I love her, is that what you want to hear?"

"I only want the truth; you can keep the rest of that bullshit. You could have just stayed away from all this drama. So it sounds like she used you as a meal ticket and you used her for a piece of ass." Phoenix spoke with an angry laugh. "Hope you learned your lesson from this, playboy, especially since you met her on Craigslist. Do you know people get killed over shit like this every single day?"

Wow, Fee you really going to a deep place tonight."

"What if I would have just snapped and fucked both of you up? Then I would be in jail over some bullshit that you started."

Marco stood in silence…stunned because he could not believe what was happening.

"So my question to you is what did she think was going to happen considering you're married?" Phoenix nodded her head, looking like she was getting much pleasure in watching Marco suffer. "You were dead wrong for leaving your marriage for a woman with three, now four kids and no future."

Marco sighed; caught up was his middle name. "This is what happened. We had sex one time that's it I promise, she called me one day and said she was pregnant and that the baby was definitely mine. That she was in love with me and wanted to start a life with me." Marco tried to explain as he leaned casually against the counter. "I panicked."

Phoenix rolled her eyes at him. "Y'all had sex one time, she gets pregnant and now she in love with you. Marco, stop with the bullshit. When I was pregnant, you made me get an abortion, but now you want to play daddy?"

"We were young back then, I told you I wasn't ready, Fee, and I meant that."

"What the fuck ever, I don't want to hear that shit. You and I are married. We were planning to have our own family and now you go play daddy and family man with someone else. You should have protected your marriage at *any* and *all* cost," Phoenix angrily shouted into Marco's face.

"She knew about you. I promise you I never denied being married, I promise."

Phoenix spoke, her tone was none too forgiving, "So is suppose to make this situation better, because it doesn't. So what did you expect from her if she knew you were in a relationship and still fucked with you? So you trust she won't do the same shit to you?"

"I don't trust her ass at all. It's crazy because my boy AJ told me I need to be the poster child for what happens when men cheat and have unprotected sex."

"He ain't lie. They need to make a Lifetime movie on this shit right here, *The Dumb Shit that Men Do*." Phoenix shook her head in disbelief.

Marco looked at Phoenix with cold eyes and an angry face. "Whatever man."

"I was your upgrade and you fuck around and downgrade yourself. You are a sorry excuse for a man. I'm glad this shit between me and you is over."

"I knew you resented me," Marco responded not truly meaning the words that just left his lips. "Look…I'm trying to do the right thing here. I'm being straight with you."

Phoenix stared at Marco with disbelief and disgust. "Trying to do the right thing, for who? Yo' selfish ass? Is it me, did I do something wrong?"

"No." Marco shook his head; he was getting frustrated with Phoenix and was beginning to regret coming.

"It has to be me," Phoenix repeated to herself. "So you don't love me anymore, you think you found someone better?" Phoenix drifted into deep thought; she shook her head after she realized she had been caught, feeling Marco's brown eyes looking directly at her.

Marco knew enough damage had been caused, so he slowly walked away from Phoenix after noticing the hurt reappear in her eyes. "Yes, of course I still love you, don't be stupid. I'm the one that's worried that you will find someone better." Marco took larger steps toward the front door, leaving Phoenix standing in front of the couch.

"I was wrong, If only you knew the real of what was going on, I'm done with this shit for right now." Marco stormed out the house, abruptly leaving Phoenix standing there holding the rest of her thoughts inside.

PHOENIX
21

It was quiet in her townhouse, something Phoenix still hadn't gotten used to since Marco no longer lived there. He moved out months ago and Phoenix missed him every day that he was gone, she loved him and wished things were different and he could be apart of her life. But he hurt her so bad, keeping her on the emotional roller coaster that he had left her on since finding out about his love child.

She looked through the mail that she had gone out to get a few minutes earlier and noticed there was mail for Marco. Seeing his name made her want to talk to him even more they needed closure; a decision had to be made in regards to their marriage. Phoenix needed to move on with her life and being married to Marco put a halt to that. At the moment Marco wasn't even talking to her, he avoided her calls sending her straight to voicemail. Phoenix stood in her kitchen she took a deep breath, she was so tired and worn out because she'd taken a lot of hits emotionally from Marco and today would be the end of all of that. With the little energy she had left, she grabbed her purse, cell phone and car keys and marched out the door to her car. She was headed to a place she never wanted to go.

The usual thirty minutes it took Phoenix to drive from her townhouse in Euclid to the Nestle Corporation in Solon where Marco worked was cut down to fifteen minutes flat. It seemed almost unreal her showing up at his job because the only time she did come there was when they had lunch dates, but today was different, she was there to confront Marco about his recent behavior. Phoenix waited in the parking lot for almost twenty minutes before she noticed Marco walking out the building, smiling, like he didn't have a care in the world. Suddenly Marco saw a figure stop directly in front of him. When he looked up and saw it was Phoenix, he got scared.

"Phoenix, this is my job, please don't come up here causing a scene. Please leave, I will be over to your house later," Marco begged, looking around at his surroundings.

"Leave!? You have a lot of nerve to allow that word to leave your lips. You just show up at my door anytime you please, then you ignore me or promise to come over to talk about our marriage and you never show up. I'm not falling for that shit again."

"Fee, please leave." Marco's face was turning red with anger because Phoenix's loud voice was now causing a scene.

"Bitch ass nigga." Phoenix spoke under her breath as she turned to walk away. She kept her face blank as she felt rain drizzling lightly on her head. She collected her thoughts and gathered up her courage.

When she heard Marco laugh, she stopped dead in her tracks and turned around. "Marco, I never hurt you. You play too many games and you're trying to drag me into your mess by showing up at my house or calling, emailing when shit over there ain't going right."

Marco tried to smile, but he just couldn't. "Look, I already told you what happened. My shit ain't happy go lucky. I made a mistake and now I have to live with it."

"You haven't told me shit but a bunch of bull. You keep saying you're going to tell me what happened or it's not what you think. When was the last time you stopped to think about how I'm feeling about this entire situation? Or how this has changed my life?"

Marco paused as if he was trying to find the right words to say. "You're talking real reckless right now."

"So you're just gon' walk away?"

"I sure am because this is not the time or place" Marco replied, walking away and not looking back after noticing that it had started raining a little bit harder. Phoenix was speechless; she was completely shocked by Marco's cold demeanor and attitude as she watched him from behind with a dumbfound expression.

"Marco wait," Phoenix pleaded as she watched Marco put his right hand into his pants pocket and slowly pull his keys out of his pocket, he unlocked the drivers side door of the truck and yanked the door open as if he was angry, slamming it shut after he slid into the drivers seat. He then pulled off his tie and laid it on the passenger seat, putting the key into the ignition to start the truck and proceeded to pull out of the parking lot of the Nestle Corporation.

Phoenix's heels clicked loudly across the parking lot as she walked briskly to her car; she pulled her keys and cell phone out of her purse and called Marco's cell phone.

"Pick the phone up, bastard!" Phoenix yelled into his voicemail. Phoenix was beyond frustrated as she took the last few steps in the direction toward her car. There were many cars in the parking lot lined up to exit so this gave her enough time to walk to her car, get in and follow behind Marco's truck which after cutting off several cars was now three cars in front of her car. The cars in front of Phoenix turned in the opposite direction which now left Phoenix directly behind Marco's truck. Phoenix put her hand out the window gesturing Marco to pull over but he ignored her gestures and continued to drive down Bainbridge road.

She was very frustrated with Marco and was now crying, she was having an out of body experience, which was the reason she wasn't paying attention that the traffic light turned red and that the Burgundy Tahoe that Marco was driving in front of her was stopping. Once Phoenix noticed he had stopped, she attempted to push down extremely hard on her breaks, but because she was driving 65 M.P.H and it was raining extremely hard, her car was going too fast to stop and she rear-ended Marco's truck.

Phoenix screamed as she heard the crunching of metal and watched pieces of glass fly everywhere

The force pushed Marco's truck into the rear of the Toyota Camry that was in front of him. The impact from Phoenix's car ejected Marco from his truck, knocking him through the front window. He was now lying on the ground between his truck and the Camry. As the realization of what just happened came to Phoenix, she jumped out her car shaking like a leaf. She felt numb, helpless and alone, she looked on the ground and saw glass everywhere.

"What did I do?" Phoenix repeated, holding her face in her hands. She ran over to the front of his truck and saw Marco lying on the ground covered in blood; she knelt down beside him and stared into his face. She was trying to take everything in. While she was gathering her thoughts, she heard a little boy screaming "Mommy, Mommy" and people began jumping out of their cars, attempting to pull the female driver out of the Camry.

"What the hell were you doing?" she heard an angry lady yell, but she didn't have the strength to respond.

"Baby! Come on, open your eyes," Phoenix screamed, tears running down her cheeks as she heard sounds of many sirens racing through the street approaching fast. She cupped his face in her hand. "Marco, get up, it's gonna be all right I promise."

Something in her chest stopped at that moment, Phoenix was certain, she could feel it. "Hang in there, baby, please hang on." Holding Marco in her arms reminded her of holding her brother Carnell in her arms years ago. The sirens from the police cars, fire trucks and ambulances grew closer and closer and now Phoenix was listening to disturbing footsteps approach her.

"Are you okay, ma'am?" the officer asked.

No matter how hard she tried, the words could not escape her lips. Phoenix nodded

"Ma'am, can you stand up and come with me? I have some questions for you"

Phoenix stood and followed the officer, but she continued to turn around, keeping her eye on Marco. The officer asked her several questions about the accident including how fast she was going and was she distracted.

Phoenix shrugged her shoulders at every question he asked her. "All I remember is I heard my car accelerate and then there was a crash," she finally responded with hesitation.

"Ma'am, do you need medical attention?"

"Am I going to be arrested?" Phoenix asked.

"Yes, you're being arrested for the cause of this accident. I need you to place your hands behind your back."

Phoenix began to panic; she had never been arrested before. Phoenix was moving her body slowly from side to side.

"Calm down, ma'am," the officer instructed.

"I am calm." Phoenix whispered as she was handcuffed and escorted to the back seat of the police car. "Please don't take me to jail," Phoenix pleaded, trying to breathe because she was now crying uncontrollably.

Phoenix was kept in interrogation room B for almost two hours; she was nervous and laid her head on the table a few times then she got up and paced around the room while waiting for the officers to question her.

"Phoenix, I'm Detective John Barnes," the older black man said as he walked in placing a note pad on the table and pulling out the chair from underneath the table. "Where were you going that had you in such a rush?" the detective asked.

"Looking for my husband."

"Do know why you're here?"

"Yes and no."

"Well let me explain, you were brought in for reckless driving and I'm just trying to get your side of the story."

"It just happened; I didn't mean to hurt anyone. It was a really bad mistake." Phoenix's voice cracked as she spoke. "I didn't see his truck stop; I didn't know the light changed. I just didn't know, I just didn't know" Phoenix repeated, banging her fist on the table.

Phoenix was booked, fingerprinted and her picture was taken then she was placed into a cell. Not long after Phoenix was arrested, she had the opportunity to call her mother. *What would I say to her? How can I explain this?* Phoenix didn't know what to expect. It was now eight o'clock in the evening and Phoenix found it hard to concentrate; she had a lot going through her mind. Thoughts of going to prison made her very afraid.

The next morning Phoenix was brought before the judge and she listened as her charges were quickly read to her. Phoenix was being charged with vehicular assault and was given a twenty thousand dollar bond.

"This can't be happening," Phoenix tried to tell her as a cold feeling suddenly swept through her body. After hearing her charges, Phoenix was then taken to the holding cell where she waited an hour to finally be taken to the county jail. She was handcuffed and crammed into a white prison van used to transport prisoners to court appearances with twelve or so other women. She took a seat on the hard wooden bench that sat on both sides of the van. It was like an animal cage, complete with cold steel bars.

Going to the county jail for the first time was a humiliating experience for Phoenix. After she was let out of the van, she was led into an area where she waited to be processed. Processing began with a strip search. Phoenix was told to walk into a room and take off all her clothes while a guard searched through her clothes and her naked body to ensure she wasn't hiding anything. After she was processed, she was given a pair of gray pants and a blue T-shirt. She was now enclosed in steel with nothing but a bed and a toilet.

The county jail was her home for the three months, the time it took her mother and friends to come up with the bond money. On her first night in the county jail, Phoenix sat up in her bunk, eyes wide, thinking about her family, friends, Marco's mother and life in general, but most of her thoughts were about Marco and the ups and downs of their lives over the last year. Phoenix knew when she married Marco her life would change

for the better but at that moment the life that she once had
with Marco, did not exist. Phoenix was trying her best to stay
calm considering her condition of being in the county jail.
Right now she felt like life was being unfair to her. Everything
around her spelled out jail, from the timed visits, the crowded
room to the limited phone time. Phoenix signed as she moved
slowly toward the hallway where the phones were located; she
picked up the phone and dialed a familiar number.

"This is AT&T, you have a collect call from the Cuyahoga
County Department of Corrections," the automated recording
spoke to Tasha

"Phoenix, I've been waiting on you to call," Tasha said
through the recording, the urgency in her voice sounding like
it didn't belong to her.

Phoenix's hand shook as she held the phone; she knew
something was wrong. "Hey sis what's going on?"

"Marco's gone." Tasha sobbed. "He's dead. He didn't make
it." Tasha cried hard; she couldn't force anymore words past her
lips.

"Tasha, tell me you're lying, how do you know? Who told
you that?" Phoenix finally managed to say, her world had
changed completely in an instant; she could feel everything
crashing in on her. She couldn't speak; the tears, rage and shock
were now locked in her throat. Phoenix's first thought was to
call his mother; they had been close ever since the day Marco
introduced them on Phoenix's first visit to New Orleans.

There was a stunned silence on the phone; Tasha took
a deep breath. "Yes, he's gone. I'm so sorry, Fee. His mother
called and told mommy" Phoenix shook her head no and then
remembered she was on the phone. "Do you want me to click
over and call his mother on three way?" Tasha asked, her voice
just as shaky as Phoenix's.

"Yeah, but I don't know what to say except I'm sorry," Phoenix replied, scared.

There was a long silence on the phone as both Tasha and Phoenix listened to the ringing of Mrs. Sutton's cell phone; the phone rang and rang until the voicemail picked up.

"Leave a message," the voice on the voicemail said.

"Mrs. Sutton, this is Phoenix, I'm so sorry." Tears took over Phoenix's words and her voice became hoarse. "This was all an accident and I never intended for anyone to get hurt. I love Marco so much. He's my husband and now I have to deal with losing him. I will try to call you later. I love you soooo much, I'm so sorry." Phoenix cried into the voicemail.

THE LAST FEW MONTHS HAD changed Phoenix more than she wanted to admit. Since being released on bail, she had been staying at her mother's house. Phoenix didn't want to stay with her mother because she hated the thought of becoming a burden…but she had no choice because she was afraid of being in the house alone.

She caught her reflection in the mirrored cabinet in the hallway at her mother's house and she was not pleased with her current look. Her hair shedding and falling out in clumps and her face breaking out like a teenager with bad acne were constant reminders that this wasn't over yet. Stress was weighing heavy on her.

"Baby, you have to eat something," her mother spoke wearing a worried look on her face while pushing past Phoenix.

"I'm not hungry," Phoenix replied. She went from weighing one hundred eighty pounds to one hundred thirty in a matter of four weeks; she didn't need a diet, stress was all the diet that she needed. She felt like she was carrying the world on her shoulders and that she could break at any moment.

"For Christ's sakes, child! That's your breakfast?" Annette cursed loud as she watched Phoenix grab the box of saltine crackers out the cabinet.

"Yeah," Phoenix replied, leaving the kitchen with the box of crackers, heading back to her own room. Phoenix closed her bedroom door and dropped to her knees, doubling over with tears. "Jesus, please protect me and give me strength to overcome this fear and pain that I'm carrying around. I've made many mistakes and I'm asking for your forgiveness of my sins." Phoenix finished her prayer and stood up, wiping her tears away.

The emptiness inside of her would not go away; she stayed in the house day and night. She lost her job with Progressive Insurance almost two months ago when she was first arrested because her story was all over the news; this left her days filled with boredom and loneliness. Phoenix could not face the world; she could no longer walk around guilt free. She felt like everyone viewed her differently. She now had a permanent record and her freedom was gone; she wouldn't be able to sit down after work and have a glass of wine or go shopping with her friends. Her thoughts were focused on her after life, life after prison.

PHOENIX
22

It had been awhile since Phoenix and her best friends
had a girl's night out. Phoenix figured since she had her
sentencing hearing in the morning, tonight would be the
perfect night for them to get together.

Phoenix moved through the crowded bar, martini glass in
hand walking toward a tall table with stools across the room.
She looked behind her, making sure Candy, Shawna, Reese,
and Tasha were still behind her. For a Tuesday night it was
packed so they all took the opportunity for the next three hours
to drink, laugh and people watch.

Finishing her drink with one deep swallow, Phoenix turned
to her friends.

"All right, I need you all to give me some words of wisdom
on surviving this shit." Phoenix looked around at all the eyes
that were focused on her; at that moment the table was silent.

"Stay away from Big Bertha," Candy the comedian of the
group blurted out.

Phoenix laughed loudly "Who?"

"Don't act like you don't know, she's the biggest bitch in
there, that's who." Candy was laughing uncontrollably; tears
began rolling down her face.

"Just stay prayed up." Reese smiled weakly trying to hold back her tears.

"Please don't come home a dyke," Shawna teased as she walked away from the table on her way to the bar. "But if you do, I will still love you anyway."

They all looked at each other in silence for a moment at Shawna's last comment, then burst out laughing. Phoenix knew the only way she was coming home a dyke was if Big Bertha raped her. Phoenix was truly enjoying this night with her friends. Ten minutes after walking away, Shawna returned to the table with five shots of tequila balanced in her hands.

"Here's to our, girl. I'm going to miss you like crazy," Shawna said, passing the shots out.

"Hold up don't drink yet, I have something I would like to add," Tasha said, tears forming in her eyes. "Fee, I love you to death, you're a great sister, daughter, friend, aunt and you were a wonderful wife. I love you." After Tasha's last words everyone swallowed their shot in one long swallow, toasting their friend before they decided to call it a night.

PHOENIX LOOKED AROUND HER TOWNHOUSE one last time to ensure that all her personal belongings were in the two boxes that she had sitting in the corner. She had made the necessary arrangements with Reese to have her townhouse cleaned out; all of her belongings would be stored in her mother's basement.

She hadn't gotten much sleep the night before; in fact, she had a horrible night. Her mind was racing a hundred miles per hour and her tearful eyes didn't help either. Her self esteem had reached its lowest point, almost non-existence, and her heart ached from missing Marco. She slumped against the wall, her hands shaking feeling as if she was out of sync with the world.

"Is this all a dream?" Phoenix pinched herself and was disappointed that what she was experiencing was indeed no dream.

Phoenix arrived at the court house at approximately 8:05 a.m.; her grandmother pulled into the parking garage across the street from the court house. Phoenix sat in the back seat of her grandmother's burgundy Cadillac, biting her nails an old habit that came out whenever she was nervous.

"Stop that!" Annette yelled, darting her eyes at Phoenix.

"My fault I'm sorry," Phoenix responded, taking a bite from the sausage McMuffin sandwich she was holding. Phoenix looked at her mother from the back seat. She was proud that her mother was now seven years clean; she no longer was on drugs or doing the negative things or hanging with the wrong people from her past. Now all Phoenix wished was that Annette would keep a job.

Phoenix, her mother and her grandmother, stepped into the elevator; Phoenix was unaware of the scene that awaited her. Her stomach was cramping and her chest tightened in a way that she could not explain. She experienced pain before, pain of all kind but nothing compared to this. No matter how hard she tried to bury it, she couldn't. Phoenix replayed the day of the accident over and over in her head a million times. She could never understand why it happened but today was her judgment day.

The elevator stopped on the third floor and all three ladies walked off and made a left turn, heading toward courtroom 18-A. Phoenix was afraid to open the wooden doors that led into the courtroom. When she finally entered, the mahogany wood benches caught her eye and the musty, damp, mildew smell that filled the air clogged her nose. Phoenix glanced around the room until her eyes came in contact with her attorney. He was on the side of the room, talking to a short man wearing a bad toupee.

When Mr. Lombardi noticed that Phoenix had walked in, he signaled for her to come over to where he was standing.

"Good morning, Mrs. Brown," Mr. Lombardi spoke, smiling, trying to ease Phoenix's mood.

"Good morning," Phoenix mumbled back.

"The gentleman I was just speaking with was Mr. Waters. He's the Assistant District Attorney. He advised me he will ask the judge to take into consideration that you don't have any prior felonies. So hopefully this will reduce your sentence to the eighteen months we previously spoke about."

Phoenix shook her head, pretending she understood and walked away to find a seat. As she sat waiting for her name to be called, it seemed as if time had slowed down and butterflies began to form in her stomach. There wasn't as many people left in the room like it had been was when she first entered so she glanced around hoping desperately to see Marco's mother. She didn't see her face amongst the group of people seated on every bench.

"Would she show up?" Phoenix asked herself as she took another look around the room. She wanted to make one last attempt before she was sentenced to apologize to Marco's mother. She felt terrible about the one and only phone call she had with his mother since the accident.

"It's all your fault!" Phoenix listened as Marco's mother screamed through the phone. "Don't bring your ass to the funeral. You're not allowed at the funeral or anywhere near my home."

"I'm so sorry, I didn't mean for this to happen," Phoenix spoke, in the back of her mind she wish there was a magic pill she could take and rewind her life back to the day she reconnected with Marco, before the infidelity.

"I hope they put your ass under the jail."

Phoenix felt like her heart had shattered into a million pieces; Marco's death was all her fault. She called his mother immediately after the accident to apologize, but she refused to talk to Phoenix. Tasha called Mrs. Sutton after Marco died, but she made it very clear that she was no longer welcomed to call. "I'm having my baby's body shipped back to New Orleans and I don't want to see none of y'all faces ever again."

Phoenix brought her attention back to the courtroom and nervously watched as the bailiff dragged in a person from behind the closed door on the side of the room. The judge began to speak "Mr. Smith, you are being charged with murder and you pleaded guilty? Is that correct?"

"Yes, that's correct, Your Honor, sir" the man in shackles and County jail clothing answered. The short cocky man, standing in front of the judge was sentenced to twenty-five years to life.

"Next case," the Judge said in a professional manner while adjusting the glasses over his eyes.

"Phoenix Brown, please step forward," the bailiff called out.

As Phoenix approached the front of the bench, she took a deep breath, mentally preparing herself for the hardest part of the day.

"Mrs. Brown, according to this document, you're charged with Involuntary Manslaughter and my records show that you have pleaded guilty to the charges. Is that correct?" the Judge asked slowly behind the thick rimmed glasses he was wearing. Unfortunately for Phoenix, Marco died shortly after she was charged with vehicular assault, so her charges were moved up to manslaughter.

"Yes, Your Honor that is correct." Phoenix replied

"Let's proceed," the judge remarked directly, laying the paper in his hand aside and clearing his throat.

Mr. Lombardi spoke, "Your Honor before we proceed, I would like to present the court with a new discovery." Phoenix snapped her neck so that she was now facing her attorney. She was caught off guard with this new so-called information and she didn't know if this information was going to hurt or help her case.

"This should have been presented before today" the judge replied, Phoenix was breathing hard; her eyes were locked on the judge.

"Your Honor, we didn't have this before today. I just received this like five minutes ago from Mr. Waters," Mr. Lombardi said, nearly pleaded.

"Mr. Waters, why wasn't this present to the court before today?" the judge questioned.

"My clerk just handed this to me and when I read the autopsy report, it was discovered that the accident that Mrs. Brown and Mr. Brown were involved in was not the direct cause of Mr. Brown's death," Mr. Waters replied. "Now she was the cause of the accident, but there was negligence at the hospital with improper use of anesthesia that caused Mr. Sutton to have a heart attack...*that* caused his death."

What the fuck, Phoenix thought as her entire body began to shake.

"This is a mess," the judge said. "So how would you like to proceed, Mr. Waters?"

"Your Honor," Mr. Lombardi said, "before he answers can I speak?"

The judge nodded, giving him permission to speak.

"My client has no previous criminal history, she's a college graduate, and she's a great woman who made a mistake. She was not seeking to cause the accident and unfortunately it happened, but she has to live with this for the reset of her life. She has to live with the fact that the future she thought she was going to have is no longer, because her husband, the man she vowed to spend her life with is no longer with us. I'm asking the court to grant Mrs. Brown with the three month time she has already served and allow her to peacefully go home and be with her family."

"Your Honor, I have no objection to that," Mr. Waters said, turning toward Mr. Lombardi and mouthing to him, "You owe me one."

"Defendant is granted credit for all time spent in custody prior to sentencing," the judge said.

Phoenix stared back at her mother, unaware that tears were forming in her eyes; she remained completely at a loss of words. Their eye contact was broken by the sound of the judge's wooden gavel sharply hitting on the bench where he sat.

Phoenix clapped a hand over her mouth to prevent herself from screaming. Her case was dropped and she was allowed to leave freely.

"Next case," the judge demanded loudly

PHOENIX WAS HAPPY SHE COULD be home with her friends and family, but she was still very angry at herself for causing the accident, angry at Marco for cheating, angry at Lourdes for not having an abortion, angry at other couples who were still together, angry at the doctors, angry at God for bringing her something so wonderful and then take it away.

Phoenix was angry at everything and everyone, she felt like the world was against her.

Marco's family had pretty much disowned her even after finding out she wasn't the direct cause of Marco's death; they treated her like she never existed. Phoenix was slightly irritated about the possible out come of the call she was about to make, she allowed her head to fall back into the couch taking in deep breaths after every digit she pushed on the phone. It's not like she didn't know how Marco's mother felt about her. It was no surprise to Phoenix, her family and Marco's family that Mrs. Sutton was disgusted with her.

Phoenix had many explanations roaming in her head as to why she couldn't, or didn't want to, call her mother-in-law. The last time they saw each other was when Phoenix flew down to New Orleans to visit Marco's grave site, Mrs. Sutton basically clawed Phoenix's eyes out as she ran Phoenix off her property after Phoenix made an unexpected visit to her house.

"Here we go" Phoenix said to herself in a calm but nerves tone as she listened to the annoying ringing. She knew Mrs. Sutton had every right to be upset with her, even if the logical side told her that it wasn't all Phoenix's fault that her son died in a tragic accident, till this day no one has ever blamed Marco for cheating and destroying their marriage, they all continued to point the finger at Phoenix and their suppose to be Christians.

Mrs. Sutton's voicemail picked up after four rings. Phoenix spoke into the voicemail, her voice tightened as she struggled through the emotional pain of leaving another unanswered phone call.

"Mrs. Sutton, this is Phoenix I'm here in New Orleans this weekend visiting Marco's grave, and I really want to talk to you face to face. You have my number, please call me. Thank you."

Phoenix really didn't expect Mrs. Sutton to call back because over the last year she hadn't answered or returned any of the repeated phone calls that Phoenix placed, except for one time and in Phoenix's mind that conversation was a disaster. Phoenix picked up on the fact that the conversation wasn't getting off to a good start based on the rude tone that Mrs. Sutton was using she was calling to ask for all of Marco's belongings. Phoenix did not want to have that conversation over the phone but at the time she wanted forgiveness so she took the little time Mrs. Sutton was given.

I'm sorry, Mrs. Sutton, but I'm not giving away any of Marco's things, not his clothes, his car, his CD collection, and I'm not turning over the money from his separate bank account to you or that baby."

"You are an evil heffa. First you kill my son now you can't help out that girl and that baby."

Phoenix took a deep breath; she was trying not to be disrespectful to her deceased husband's mother, but Mrs. Sutton was pissing her off. "Mrs. Sutton, this is a daily struggle for me; I get by the best way I can, but you have never called to ask me how I was feeling. I know what happened to your son, remember I was there and I'm hurting. I'm not the same person I used to be, I have to live with his death each and every day. I have no motivation to do *anything*. Marco was the love of my life, I knew from the moment we met up again that I would love him for the rest of my life. Your son created this mess." Phoenix spoke without even breathing. "It's horrible that, the baby will not know her father but I will not help out I can't do that; if you want help for that baby then you help out." Phoenix had tears rolling down her face uncontrollably, the conversation she was having with Mrs. Sutton was just way too much for her and she wanted this call to end really soon.

"I take care of my grandbaby."

"Why didn't Lourdes call me with this mess, she sent you to handle her dirty work? We don't even know if that's his child. It's not my fault they didn't get a paternity test or that he didn't sign the birth certificate.

"No one has me doing their dirty work; I'm doing this for my grandbaby. They were in the process of having that done... Missy," Mrs. Sutton hollered through the phone.

"Well why didn't Marco sign the birth certificate at the hospital? That's because he had doubts. Listen, I'm not trying to be rude, but I'm still grieving the loss of my husband, and I don't need all this added stress."

Mrs. Sutton stumbled over her words. "I'm grieving, too. I will take you to court and fight you for his stuff."

"Take me to court, I don't care anymore because it seems like you have too much time on your hands to be grieving and I'm trying to move on with my life. We were still married when he died. I'm his wife. I already let you have a funeral that I was not present at, and then you have my husband buried thousands of miles away from me." Phoenix spoke, not stopping for air between her words. "And now you're calling me about his belongings."

"You're selfish, just selfish, walking around with my son's entire life savings. Yeah, I know he had some insurance policies and you can't even help out that baby."

"Help out the baby? You're not going to let that go, even after I already told you I wasn't doing that." Phoenix was becoming frustrated with this conversation, but she wasn't about to let Mrs. Sutton know. "Your son left everything to me. I was still the beneficiary on all his paperwork and bank accounts, so I'm entitled to *everything*."

"He shouldn't have left you shit because you don't deserve it."

"Oh, thank you, but he did. Mrs. Sutton, that's your personal opinion, but answer me this—when is your family going to place some blame on Marco because he was the cause of all of this?" Phoenix never received the answer to her question because without saying a word Mrs. Sutton slammed down the phone and hadn't picked up since. All Phoenix wanted to know was why? Why wasn't anyone blaming Marco or Lourdes for all of this. Why did she have to take complete blame…was it because Marco was no longer alive?

PHOENIX SAT IN HER CAR, silently looking out the window at the thick cloud that blocked out the sun and when she stepped out the car, the biting cold wind slapped her face. As she maneuvered her way up the path to Marco's grave site, she jumped when she heard the wrought iron gate screeched as it swung back and forth from the old rusty hinges from the wind blowing against it.

She looked around the overly packed graveyard until she walked up on Marco's gravestone. The words his mother chose to have written on the headstone read *Loving Husband, Son and Father*. It had been almost a year since Phoenix last laid eyes on Marco, but it seemed like yesterday. She shut her eyes for a moment and tears began falling as she stepped closer and closer to his grave. With every step she took, more tears slid down her face, she finally reached his grave and stood staring at the ground for a moment before falling to her knees. Phoenix gently brushed away the dirt and rocks as she traced the letters and numbers that were engraved in the stone.

Phoenix continued to look at the headstone as she spoke. "I truly love, I really love you, I gave you my life, my all and you turned around and hurt me, your family and my family. Now there is a child that will never know you. She will never know the silly, caring, loving protector that I once knew." She paused to gather her thoughts "Marco, I was partly responsible for you no longer being here, but I would give anything to trade places with you."

Phoenix sat on the ground crying without saying a word; when she stood to leave she felt a rush of warm air brush past her.

"I knew you always had my back." She smiled, putting on her BEBE sunglasses and walking back to her rental car. When she opened the car door she said, "The outer surface only shows a portion of me, what lies beneath is what really matters." Phoenix cried uncontrollably as she got behind the wheel and drove away.

ACKNOWLEDGEMENTS

God, my Father, I thank You for creating me and loving me. Thank you for all You do and all You have to give.

Writing *Unexpected Truth* was a personal journey of self improvement. I've learned that no matter how bad things may seem, there is always something to be more thankful for. There are so many people that I would like to thank for their love and support. I can't mention everyone's name personally, but know that you're in my heart. Thank you for supporting me every step through this journey. It's been tough, but I made it through. All of your encouraging words meant so much to me.

Sheldonia Sidberry, you make me laugh, you make me cry and you make me smile. Thank you for being my sister/friend. I'm still working on getting you out to Hollywood because the stars are all around you. I love you.

Brittany Tardy, you always amaze me. When you smile you brighten the room with your cheerful personality. I cherish our friendship very much. Thanks for the support. I love you, Bee.

Rodney G., thanks for having my back on the days I just knew I had no more energy to fight this battle. You know exactly what to say and when to say it. I truly appreciate our friendship.

Verlene Drake, you love me like your own and I am forever grateful. Thank you.

Tashauna Johnson, you're my newest friend out of the bunch but our bond is just as strong as the rest. When I relocated I thought it would be impossible finding a friend but I managed to find you. Thank you for all your support, many laughs and just the genuine love and friendship.

Geri Tyes, God has something mighty prepared for you, so prepare yourself for the greatness that's coming your way. I love you and I cherish our relationship. It can never be replaced. Your smile makes the world move.

Tequila Pennington-Calwise, our friendship expands over twenty-six years. There have been many times when life took us on different paths, but the friendship has always remained. I love you and thank you for been a wonderful friend.

Dr. Sashelle Alexander, I'm so proud of your accomplishments I've had the pleasure of walking through this journey of life with you and I thank God that I was able to experience so many memories with you. You inspire me to become a better person. Thank you for my nephew Ean it's a joy watching him grow into a young man. I love you both.

Shelly Reynolds, not only can I call you my sister, but also my friend. I've cried on your shoulder many times, and not once did you push me away. Thank you for always being in my corner. You are a beautiful and great sister. I love you.

Hiram Bey, I can't thank you enough for your continuous love, support and encouragement. It means so much to have such a wonderful man as my father.

Vernell Bey (RIP), mommy you are my hero and the reason I'm who I am today. You were the strongest woman I've ever met and I want to be just like you when I grow up.

Thank you to my friends, family, book stores and book clubs. It's been a while but I truly appreciate your support in reading my books.

Much Love,

Makenzi

ABOUT THE AUTHOR

Makenzi is the author of three fiction novels, *That's How I like It!*, *Dangerously* and her newest novel *Unexpected Truth*. She is a from Cleveland, Ohio, but currently lives in the Hampton Roads area of Virginia.

VYSS Publishing

Visit us online:
www.authormakenzi.blogspot.com

Made in the USA
Charleston, SC
11 April 2014